MARIONETTE

"The fascinating study of sex used as a weapon for manipulative power like Dangerous Liaisons entwined with the wickedly clever use of seances and hypnosis as the erotic arena in which these evil manipulations are carried out. Antonia Rachel Ward had me in the palm of her hand."
—Sadie Hartmann, co-editor of *Human Monsters*, a horror anthology, and editor-in-chief at Dark Hart Books.

"A startling blend of genres that I sincerely hope to see much more of, Marionette is gripping, thrilling, titillating, and simply beautiful. If you don't want to live and breathe fin de siècle Paris and mingle with stars, hypnotists, and phantoms at erotic seances, I don't know how to help you."
—Alex Woodroe, editor, Romanian folkore nerd, and author of *Whisperwood*.

Evocative of Angela Carter in the way it blends the horrific with the erotic, Marionette is a vivid and vivacious read which satisfies on more levels then one.
—April Yates, author of *Ashthorne*.

Marionette

by
Antonia Rachel Ward

Edited by Elle Turpitt.
Proofread and formatted by Stephanie Ellis

Cover illustration and design by Daniella Batsheva
www.daniellabatsheva.com
First Edition: August 2022

ISBN (paperback): 978-1-957537-27-6
ISBN (Kindle ebook): 978-1-957537-26-9
Library of Congress Control Number: 2022937447

BRIGIDS GATE PRESS
Bucyrus, Kansas
www.brigidsgatepress.com

Printed in the United States of America

For Emily

Content warnings are provided at
the end of this book.

PRELUDE

"In the forest, a long time ago, lived spirits who would dance a man to death. Beneath the light of a full moon, the ghosts of spurned women rose from their beds of earth and moss to charm unwary travelers into their embrace. They spared no man, no matter how innocent a life he had led.

"To the wraiths, all men were the same: treacherous, untrustworthy. Unworthy of life. Any fool who stumbled into their clutches found himself forced to dance with them the whole night long, until at last he expired from sheer exhaustion. Only if he could make it to sunrise—when the spirits were forced to disperse—would he survive."

"Did any of them ever survive?" Cece had asked, the last night she saw her aunt.

Marthe shook her head, her eyes glittering in the firelight.

"No, Cece. Not one." She got to her feet and kissed her little niece on the top of her head. "Thank heaven for small mercies."

CHAPTER ONE

George Dashwood woke with a start as a screech of brakes heralded the arrival of the Normandy train. The engine let off a whistle of steam into the smoke-clogged rafters of the Gare Saint Lazare, where it billowed like a grubby rain cloud in its own tiny weather system. The other passengers in the compartment were already on their feet, shrugging on coats, tugging down suitcases from the luggage rack, unfurling umbrellas.

Paris! Could it really be? It seemed like no time at all since George had alighted from the Portsmouth ferry, face stinging with the cold saltwater air. A few hours chugging along the tracks, and here he was: the city of light. A wonderful invention, these railways.

He snatched up his hat and fixed it as best he could over his unruly hair. Then, grabbing his case, he followed the others out of the carriage. Smoke stung his eyes and tickled the back of his throat as he wove through the throng and headed out onto the wet pavement. Wishing he'd brought an umbrella himself, he gazed at the tall, soot-covered buildings, the dark-suited clerks hurrying by in the evening drizzle. It could have been London. Surely Paris held something more exotic than this?

Across the plaza, a man on a ladder attempted to light a gas streetlamp, the flame flaring and dying in the damp breeze. George withdrew a crumpled piece of paper from his pocket, hunching over to read it before raindrops blurred the ink. His friend's hand-drawn map left a little to be desired. He turned the paper around in his hands, puzzling over it, and at last set out along a broad boulevard.

Shop windows shone invitingly in the fading light, like golden sweet wrappers hiding treasures within. George passed pharmacies full of colored bottles of lavender water, and patisseries piled high with delicate sugar confections. In one window, a white sugar swan reared up, wings outstretched as if to batter down the window and escape onto the street. Carriages trundled along the cobbles, while gentlemen in top hats escorted ladies with bustled skirts that bobbed as they walked. George turned to watch one such lady pass by, momentarily distracted by the tightness of her gown and the dainty steps she took as she tottered along on the arm of her companion.

He'd heard stories of the Parisian women, of course, when he and Bastian were at boarding school together: "Oh, the girls, Georgie! You must come and meet our girls! They are beyond compare." To hear Bastian tell it, the entire city was rampant with insatiable prostitutes and predatory widows with a taste for young male flesh.

George chuckled, recalling how he must have looked, mouth open in amazement, fairly panting at the thought of so many delectable women. Now, having turned nineteen, he was not as entirely unworldly as he'd been a year ago. He was determined to forgo—or at least, keep to a minimum—the attractions of Bastian's fabled girls, the better to focus on his painting. George's father had agreed to fund his trip on the condition that he was here to learn, not fritter his time away on women. If he wanted to eat, he must keep his promise. *Never mind how pretty they are,* he reminded himself, turning to watch another rosy-cheeked delight go by.

George rounded a corner to face the over-decorated wedding cake that was the new Palais Theatre. In front of it stood a cart laden with flowers, its owner advertising bouquets to passing theatre-goers. As George consulted his rain-blotted map once more, he noticed a figure running towards him across the plaza, and the next thing he knew, he was pulled into an enthusiastic embrace.

"Georgie, old chum!" Bastian exclaimed, in perfect English. "I feared you would not make it in time. Come, come! If we want a decent seat, we must make haste."

"The theatre?" George fell into step beside his friend. "I've been travelling all day. A decent dinner and a warm bed appeal to me rather more, I must say."

"Ah, but you don't understand." Bastian stopped beside the flower-seller and ordered two large bouquets. "All will become clear when you see her."

"Who?"

Smiling, Bastian deposited one of the bouquets in George's arms. "You'll see. Ask for your name to be put on the card, and we'll leave them at the stage door with your luggage before we go in."

Bastian, Duc d'Armand, led George Dashwood, Esq., son of nobody much worth mentioning, around to the stage door, only a touch less grand than the theatre's main entrance. There, he passed the bouquets to a porter.

"For Cecile," he instructed, and the porter laughed.

"I'll put them with the rest."

"Cecile?" George asked, but before Bastian could answer, a gentleman in a red velvet coat approached them, striding up to the door quite as if he owned the place. Jeweled rings bedecked his fingers, and he carried a silver-topped cane.

"Monsieur le Duc," he said, tipping his hat to Bastian.

"Rossignol, old fellow!" Bastian raised his eyebrows. "Is the Comte here tonight?"

"Not tonight." Rossignol smiled, his eyes crinkling above his full beard. "Tonight, I am safe. I shall be entertaining later, Monsieur le Duc. Do come… and bring your friend."

As the gentleman disappeared inside, George caught Bastian's eye.

"Flamboyant looking fellow."

"Rather the eccentric, it's true. But his parties are legendary."

"Parties?"

Bastian waved the question away, leading the way to the theatre's main entrance, where the clamor of the crowd swallowed George's attempts at further conversation. Instead, he took in the Palais Theatre's breathtaking grand staircase. Reflections from the chandeliers shone on the polished marble floor, while ladies in flounced dresses adorned every step like overgrown flowers. Bastian showed him into the auditorium, where the air was hot with the bated breath of an audience of hundreds.

"Sevigny must be making a fortune from this girl," he commented. "No wonder Rossignol's hanging around. I suppose he wants a piece of the action."

The place was crammed well above capacity. Gentlemen in top hats and cravats stood shoulder-to-shoulder down the aisles while ladies filled every last seat. Dragging George behind him, Bastian forced his way into a place in the front row, close enough to the stage that George could feel the heat of the footlights on his face. His cheeks glowed; he sweated profusely beneath his winter coat. Crushed between Bastian and another eager-eyed gentleman, he took off his hat and ran a hand through his damp hair as the orchestra struck up.

The hubbub fell to a murmur, but amongst the hushed voices one name was audible, repeated over and over as the lights dimmed and the curtain rose.

Cecile.

In the low, flickering light, a group of dancers scampered onto the dark stage—a cloud of white dresses, shapely calves just visible underneath. They fluttered around and between each other in a rustle of skirts, weaving patterns, looking as otherworldly as ghosts. Even the softest breeze could have scattered them to the wind like dandelion seeds, if it hadn't been for the steady thumping of their feet, exposing them as all too real. They were pretty feet, though, and for a while, George got lost in studying them, until Bastian nudged him hard in the ribs.

"There she is."

A girl in blue silk darted into the spotlight, accompanied by an explosion of applause. Here, crowned with flowers, was the girl they'd all come to see.

"Cecile Dulac," Bastian muttered. "A fresh little blossom, just arrived in the city. Everyone wants her."

At first, George couldn't understand it. Even playing the part of Venus, Goddess of Love, there was something of the milkmaid about Cecile. Her arms were thick, her skin mottled with a blush that spread from her chest to her cheeks. Her bountiful breasts threatened to spill out of her tight bodice. There was nothing ethereal about her. Yet, as he watched, George began to find her somehow beguiling, with her caramel hair and forget-me-not blue eyes. It was the sensuous way she danced. The slight sway of her torso; the delicate curl of her wrist; the way she glanced over her shoulder as she turned away, flirting with the audience as if she were calling a man to bed.

He imagined painting her, tracing the swan-like curve of her neck and shoulders with his pencil, filling in the expanse of her décolletage with his brush. Cecile on canvas in oils. He leaned forward, craning his neck to get a better look.

"Mon Dieu, I think he likes her!" Bastian chuckled. "After the performance, I'll take you backstage and introduce you. You would like that, no?"

"No." George tried, and failed, to drag his eyes away from the vision in front of him. "No. I need to retire to my rooms and sleep. I'm not here for merrymaking. I promised my father I would work at my art."

"Ah, Dashwood, but art is not work. It is life! And what better way to experience life than to spend some time with a beautiful girl? You will come. You must promise."

On the stage, Cecile Dulac snaked her hips from side to side, undulating with the music, and shot a glance—it seemed—right at George. Her full lips twitched with an enchanting smile. George sighed.

"Very well," he said. "I will come."

CHAPTER TWO

At the end of the final act, a flurry of celestial beings crossed the threshold of the stage and returned to their earthly state. Cece stopped running the moment she was out of the audience's sight, and bent double, hands on her knees, waiting for her breath to return. One of her fellow dancers tossed her a napkin, and she dabbed the sweat from her forehead and chest, smearing the white fabric with stage makeup.

"Lord, what a crowd," she exclaimed, under cover of the applause. "Packed to the rafters. I wouldn't have thought so many people would fit if I hadn't seen it for myself!"

"Yes, and all of them here for you, Cece," Rosie replied, grasping Cece's shoulders and turning her around. "Get back out there and give them what they want."

Cece laughed. "I know what they want, and it's not a curtsy."

Beaming, she darted out beneath the hot stage lights to absorb the adoration of the audience. Flowers gathered around her feet, tossed by the gentlemen in the front rows. A boy scurried over and placed an overflowing bouquet of red roses in her arms. Cece dropped one curtsy after another, glancing up at the boxes around the sides of the auditorium, trying to make out the faces in the darkness. Monsieur Rossignol was here tonight, somewhere in those shadows, and she wanted to be sure he'd seen her.

When finally the curtain fell, she stood in the dimming spotlight, unwilling to move. She wanted to hold onto the moment. Wrap it around her like a warm cloak, to protect her from the chilly reality that would greet her the moment she stepped off stage. The reality in which she was not the glamorous Cecile Dulac, star of the Palais Theatre, but plain, ordinary Cece, a country girl who'd once sucked farmhands' cocks for enough sous to buy bread. What would they say, she wondered, if they could see her now?

Probably spit at my feet and call me whore. There was a reason she'd walked out of that village the night her mother died, and never looked back.

"Will you look at her with all her flowers!" A petite dancer accosted Cece as she returned to the wings, with a smile that was half a sneer. "What is it you've got that I don't, I wonder?"

"She's got a chest, for a start," laughed Rosie. "Look at 'em. I'd like to get my hands on 'em myself."

"I don't doubt it, Rosie." Cece passed her flowers to a nearby stagehand. "We all know what you get up to."

"You know nothing." Rosie stuck her nose in the air, but there was a shadow of a smile on her face. She was brown-skinned and pink-lipped, with eyes dark enough to drown in, but her inner arms were pockmarked with round, silvery scars about which she refused to speak.

"You think we haven't heard about those parties you go to?" Cece raised her eyebrows as the girls made their way through the stomach of the building, to the foyer where they would greet their patrons. "Monsieur Rossignol's parties? I may not have been here long, but it's long enough to hear the gossip."

"Uh huh. And wouldn't you love to know if it's all true?" Rosie slipped an arm around the shorter girl's waist, leaning in close enough to whisper in her ear. "You could come with me tonight. Monsieur's guests would just adore a sweet little country bumpkin like you. All bright-eyed and innocent. They would just eat you up."

Her lips brushed Cece's earlobe, soft as flower petals, making her skin tingle. She shivered and pulled away from Rosie's grasp, covering her confusion with a hearty laugh.

"Innocent? Me?" Cece glanced at the other girls, and they laughed along with her. "Come on now, Rosie. My old mother put me on the job when I hardly knew how to tie my own ribbons. Reading tarot cards for superstitious ladies in the market square by day, fucking their husbands round the back of the tavern by night. How else d'you think we made a living?"

As she spoke, they entered the foyer—a room opulent far beyond anything Cece could have conceived during her days in the alley behind the tavern. Every time she set foot in there, with its painted ceiling and blazing chandeliers, she felt as though she had stepped into a fairy tale.

The place was filling up with gentlemen—*abonnés*, as the girls' patrons were known—and despite their exhaustion and hunger after a long performance, the dancers were expected to remain on their feet and be charming. Keeping the abonnés happy kept the theatre running, or so the owner, the Comte du Sevigny, liked to tell them, on the rare occasions he attended their rehearsals in person.

"So you've had your holes filled," Rosie replied, in a low voice. "But what of *pleasure*?"

Cece snorted. "What man knows how to please a woman? For that matter, what man cares? They have their way and then they're done. That's all there is to it."

"Whoever said I was talking about men? Come with me tonight. You won't be sorry. You're welcome just to watch, this time, but if you choose to join me on stage, Monsieur will make sure you're well compensated, I promise."

"On stage?" Cece repeated, her attention piqued, but Rosie only smiled, glancing at the door opposite.

"If Sevigny sees *him* here, there will be trouble," she whispered. "Let us hope he does not."

Cece followed her gaze. There in the doorway, Monsieur Rossignol himself had materialized. He stood out in his red jacket against the black and white of the other abonnés, not quite handsome, but magnetic, with his sharp cheekbones and blue-green eyes.

When he spotted Rosie, he made his way over, and the crowd parted ahead of him, as though they were mere extras in a performance belonging to him alone. Cece, suddenly nervous, had the urge to scurry away and hide herself in a dark corner. Instead, she plastered on a smile—the same smile that had worked on Sevigny to win her the lead role in his new show. Would it work as effectively on Rossignol, she wondered, and convince him to let her attend his party? As he lifted her hand to his lips and kissed it, she gave herself permission to hope it might.

"Mademoiselle Dulac. A pleasure to meet you." He spoke softly, his eyes never leaving hers.

Under his intense, unblinking gaze, she could have been the only woman in the room. It was both flattering and discomfiting. Many men undressed Cece with their eyes, but he… he seemed to want to peel her skin back and expose the vulnerable, pulsing heart beneath. She wasn't at all sure she liked it, but she dropped a curtsy anyhow, doing her best to look charmed. If an innocent country girl was what Rossignol wanted, then an innocent country girl was what she would be. She dipped her gaze bashfully, then raised it again, as if she found him so attractive she couldn't resist snatching another glance.

Letting go of Cece's hand, he slipped a proprietary arm around Rosie's waist, then addressed Cece again. "I have a proposal for you, Mademoiselle Dulac. Perhaps you would be good enough to entertain me in your dressing room, so we may discuss it in private."

His words were formal, but his eyes twinkled. Cece pretended to hesitate, looking to Rosie as if for encouragement. In truth, she needed no encouragement. She already knew that Rossignol's 'girls' received special treatment. Rosie and the others, with their fine new clothes and jewels, were revered and respected by their peers, despite—or perhaps because of—the rumors about what they got up to at Monsieur's parties. People called Rossignol the Prince of Debauchery, and Cece was willing to find out why, if it meant she could wear real furs and drive everywhere in a hansom cab. She let him take her waist with his free arm, and the three of them walked out of the foyer together.

CHAPTER THREE

Sharing a bottle of wine in the foyer, George and Bastian watched Rossignol leave with the two girls. Bastian downed the last of his drink and grasped George's arm.

"Dashwood! Come on! We're going backstage."

He dragged George along, weaving his way through the throng to an unobtrusive door, where they ducked into a bare-walled corridor several degrees cooler—and considerably quieter—than the foyer.

"Are we allowed to be back here?" George asked.

Bastian grinned. "You worry too much, old chap. The owner's an old family friend. The Comte is unlikely to turn me out."

With the air of a seasoned explorer, Bastian navigated the rabbit warren of corridors until they came to a peeling, blue-painted door. He knocked smartly, and a woman's voice called, "Who is it?"

"The Duc d'Armand."

"Well, come in!"

The windowless room smelled of stale sweat covered by a faint scent of rosewater. Faded, red flocked wallpaper gave the place a comforting atmosphere. There were half-a-dozen girls in there, wandering around in various states of undress, but only one man— Monsieur Rossignol.

He lounged on a threadbare sofa in his shirtsleeves, arms spread across the back of the chair, one ankle hooked over the other leg. His silver-topped cane leant against the arm of the sofa, beside his discarded jacket. He gave a nod of recognition to Bastian, then turned his attention back to the girls.

Some of them were half out of their costumes, one bending over in her short, tulle skirt while she helped another to unlace her bodice. Others had already changed into their pantaloons and chemises, apparently undeterred by Rossignol's presence. Skin was on show everywhere: calves, bare arms, décolletages. It was even possible, George couldn't help but notice, to see some of the girls' nipples underneath the thin fabric of their chemises.

But the one who really drew his eye was Cecile Dulac, standing at her dressing table in her Venus costume, pulling pins from her hair. She glanced over her shoulder to acknowledge their entrance with a dazzling smile.

"Monsieur le Duc." She greeted Bastian in French, placing her pins down amongst the little glass bottles and combs on her dressing table. "What a pleasure to see you again."

Her accent had a rough, country edge, not completely hidden by the veil of sophistication she tried to draw over it. Somehow that made George like her all the more. She was so fresh compared with the stuffy society girls he knew in London.

"Please, no need to be so formal," Bastian said. "Here I'm simply Bastian."

Cecile let her caramel hair fall down in waves around her shoulders and turned to face him. "Here you may be the king of Persia, if you so choose."

"I choose only to be your servant, Madame," Bastian replied, with a deep bow.

"And this gentleman?"

"My dear friend, George Dashwood."

"Ah! English!" Cecile switched to English, which she spoke with her hands clasped in front of her, like a schoolgirl reciting from memory. "Mr. Dashwood, I delight in making your acquaintance."

"The pleasure is all mine," George replied in French. The hint of relief in Cecile's smile made his heart swell. She shot him a glance that seemed to say: *You understand me a little better than these others, I can tell.*

"Gentlemen," Rossignol called. "Please, sit down and have some wine. Rosie!"

He beckoned to a girl with light brown skin and dark ringlets, who poured red wine into two glasses perilously balanced on Cecile's dressing table. George and Bastian sat on the sofa, and Rosie passed them the glasses with a wink. She giggled when Rossignol responded with a pat on her rump.

Smiling, he turned to Bastian. "I haven't seen you in a while, Monsieur le Duc. How do you like Sevigny's new girl?"

"I like her very much." Bastian's eyes strayed to Cecile, who was taking delivery of a vast bouquet of roses from a stagehand at her door. "But my friend here likes her even better, I think. He has just arrived in France, and I wanted to show him the best we have to offer."

"Indeed, indeed!" Rossignol fixed his gaze on George, who had the feeling that beneath the bonhomie, he was being studied in much the same way as a cat might study a mouse. "I shall be holding a little soirée tonight, Mr. Dashwood, for select customers only. It costs only a small fee to attend. You seem a discerning fellow. Perhaps you might like to join us?"

George pushed aside his distaste at the thought of charging a fee for a 'soirée' and merely nodded, turning his attention back to Cecile, who had placed the roses on her dressing table. Plucking the card from their midst, she waved it beneath Rosie's nose.

"Another from the Comte du Sevigny," she said, in a stage whisper audible to everybody in the room. "What a bore he is. He's sent me roses every day this week. If he thinks that'll earn a space for his boots under my bed, he'll have to think again." And she cackled—an uninhibited, dirty laugh that sent a little thrill through George's spine.

Flashing a sweet smile at the gentlemen, Cecile gestured to Rosie for help with her costume. George tried not to watch too overtly as Rosie unlaced her bodice and Cecile fidgeted and stretched, arching her back and her shoulders.

"Lord! How uncomfortable these things are. I can hardly wait to get it off. You tied it far too tight, Rosie."

"You want it tight, Cece," Rosie replied, pausing in her unlacing to place her hands on Cecile's waist. "Nice and tight, to show off this beautiful figure."

As she spoke, she moved her hands up, slowly, until they cupped Cecile's breasts. Then Cecile cast a glance at the men watching, and the two girls dissolved into laughter.

George thought of the young ladies his mother invited to the house, trying to tempt him into choosing a wife. Ladies in frilled lace who sat straight-spined and smiled wanly while they sipped tea from china cups. Pale girls with sad eyes and colorless cheeks. Cecile's face was flushed pink with the heat of the room, her eyes sparkling and alive. When she finished laughing, she turned to survey the men, hands on her hips, a tiny smile curling the corners of her mouth.

"Are you gentlemen going to sit there and watch me undress?"

"With pleasure, Mademoiselle." Bastian sat back, hooking one ankle over the other knee. George shot him a glare, but Cecile only laughed.

"Monsieur le Duc, what a cad you are." Bodice loosened, she wriggled a little, until one of the straps slipped from her shoulder. "I really must have some privacy while I change. You boys ought to run along. But you will go to Monsieur Rossignol's party later, won't you?"

"Cece will be the star attraction," Rosie added, kissing her friend's neck, then glancing up at them with a smile.

George looked at Rossignol. The man's cold stare made his skin crawl. Exactly what did he have in mind for Cecile at this party?

"It's late," George began. "I ought to find my lodgings. It's my first night in Paris, you know…"

"Well!" Rossignol cut in. "What better reason to join us? Start as you mean to go on. Monsieur le Duc?"

"I would not miss it for all the world. Georgie, old chap, how can you possibly refuse? Look how you have disappointed Mademoiselle Dulac."

Mademoiselle Dulac pouted prettily, blinking her round blue eyes. "I am bereft, Monsieur Dashwood," she agreed, "if you do not join us."

She wandered over to her pile of bouquets and ran a finger over one of her red roses, probing its velvety petals. Plucking it from its fellows, she raised it to her nose.

"Ouch!"

"What is it, Cece?" Rosie turned to her.

"This thorn pricked me." Cecile held up a finger, showing a scarlet bead of blood that stood out against her ivory skin.

"Poor baby." Rosie plucked the rose from her hand. "Does it hurt much?"

"A little."

"Let me kiss it better." Rosie took Cecile's hand and, with a tiny smile, popped the bloodied finger into her mouth. She withdrew it slowly, leaving a hint of red on her bottom lip, which she licked off with a fleck of her pink tongue.

"Much better," Cecile purred.

Whores. In the back of his mind George heard his father's voice. Paris is full to the brim with them. Filthy sluts and liars, every one. They'll take your money and your sense and leave you lying in the gutter, addled with laudanum. Art! You won't come back with a sketch to your name.

George had sworn to prove him wrong. He meant to apply himself solely to his art, without distractions, and return with something to be proud of. Some sales. An exhibition of his own, perhaps. *They'll leave you lying in the gutter, addled with laudanum.*

But Cecile was so young, so angelic. Surely she was not capable of such behavior? Not unless she was led astray by the people around her. As Rosie drew Cecile closer and kissed her full on the lips, the danger she was in struck George with a force that jarred his nerves. How could he leave her unprotected, at their mercy? Who knew what Rossignol had in mind for her at this party of his? No, he must go. That much was clear. There was time enough to study, once he'd satisfied himself that Cecile was safe. Tomorrow he would begin in earnest.

CHAPTER FOUR

Cece fanned herself with an ostrich feather, slouching in her seat as Monsieur Rossignol's carriage trundled through the cobbled streets of Paris. She was light-headed with nerves, her stomach fluttering.

The street lamps threw long shadows across the stone façades of the townhouses, turning their blank windows into glinting eyes.

"You laced me up too tightly again, Rosie," she complained. "I can barely breathe."

Rosie rolled her eyes. "Oh, Cece, must you moan so very much?"

She sat alongside Rossignol in a pale pink evening gown, while Cece, in blue, rode opposite them, her pile of bouquets taking up the space beside her.

"I shall moan as much as I please. I'm sure I'm quite ready to pass out."

"Try not to, Mademoiselle, or at least not yet." Rossignol shot her a smile, his blue-green eyes cold as ice-water.

Cece shivered. The way her fellow dancers talked about him, one would think he had the power of life and death over them. His approval meant fame, riches, respect. His disapproval... Well, she hadn't gleaned any specifics, but she'd heard whispers. Girls who had been particular favorites of his, who'd been there one night and gone the next. His mysterious feud with the Comte du Sevigny. And then there was Rosie and her scars. But Cece was no stranger to risk. When you relied on men to help you make your way in the world, there was always a risk.

"You still haven't told me what part I'll be playing tonight," she said. "How shall I know what to do, if you won't tell me?"

"You'll know, don't worry."

"Quite some star I'll be, bumbling around with no idea what the show even is!" Cece forced a laugh, looking out at the lamps lining the dark boulevard. Men and women in their evening clothes strolled by, leaving restaurants and theatres, heading for late-night parties and balls. "I wonder if I shouldn't just watch this evening? I've already been on stage once tonight. I'm dreadfully tired."

"Mademoiselle, what is that in your hair?" Rossignol leaned forward, reaching for the concoction of curls and feathers atop Cece's head. When he withdrew his hand, he held something dark red and sparkling, which he handed to her.

"What is this?" Cece examined the jewel, trying not to let her delight show. It was the size of a coin, and her face reflected over and over in its facets. A black velvet ribbon hung from its silver setting. "For me?"

"For you," said Rossignol. "A ruby. Put it on. Let me see how it brings out the color in your cheeks."

Cece tied the choker around her throat and turned her head this way and that, trying to glimpse her reflection in the window glass. Her face stared back at her, flickering and ghostly pale, but the necklace stood out clear and bright in the darkness, as though it shone from within.

"It's beautiful," she sighed. These days it was hardly unheard of for men to give her jewelry, but this was by far the biggest and most extravagant piece she'd received. Why, even her rich Aunt Marthe would surely have been impressed by this jewel—if only Cece knew where she was now.

But Cece had searched for Marthe ever since her arrival in Paris, and nobody seemed to have heard of her. All the letters Marthe had sent home, describing her rise to stardom as a dancer in the Palais; her marriage to one of the city's wealthiest noblemen—had they all been lies, after all? It was because of those letters that Cece had left her village and walked all the way to Paris, seeking to follow in Marthe's footsteps. Perhaps, as it turned out, she was walking in the footsteps of a fairy tale.

It hardly mattered now. Cece wriggled her shoulders with delight as she sank deeper into the luxurious carriage seats. She was living the very myth her aunt had sold to her.

Soon, the carriage rolled to a halt in front of the Chateau Rossignol, close to the banks of the Seine. The palace was fronted with golden stone and more windows than Cece could count. Above the door, a carved figurehead looked down—a woman's face and torso, her long hair flowing loose over her shoulders, her breast bare.

A footman opened the carriage door, and Rossignol helped Cece and Rosie out onto the driveway. The party had begun without them, music pouring from the chateau's open door, light spilling onto its stone steps.

Cece fingered her new necklace as they headed inside. Then, remembering she was supposed to be a fine lady now, she dropped her hand and turned on her best smile for the guests gathered in the marble-floored entrance hall. Their eyes followed her like spotlights as they whispered her name like an incantation. *Cecile. Cecile!*

Even more pairs of eyes waited in the ballroom, where guests waltzed in time to a string quartet. In the mirrored walls, reflections caught reflections, vanishing into infinity, making it difficult to see where reality ended and the mirror-world began. It was as though the party went on forever. That it might just continue, in that ghostly world, even after everyone had left, and the ballroom was empty and dark.

"Look over there." Rosie pointed to a group of young men lounging in a corner. "It's the Duc d'Armand and that boy he brought along with him."

Cece laughed. "The poor child," she said, even though she was sure he must be older than her.

When the Comte du Sevigny had plucked her off the street and let her stand at the back of the rehearsal room, copying the moves of the older dancers, Cece had learned more than just the steps— she had also learned to affect a degree of worldly ennui that all the girls carried everywhere they went. To be a lady in Paris you had to act as though nothing moved you, nothing impressed you. And so, when she saw a vast ballroom full of wealthy people in fine clothes and jewels, or a group of rich men who all wanted to be her suitor, Cece quashed the excitement that threatened to bubble up inside her and pretended to find it all intensely dull. Somehow, it seemed to work. People liked her. Admired her. Men worshiped at her feet. One day they would find her out as the simple country girl she really was, and the bubble would burst, and it would all be over. But until then she would pretend, for as long as she was able.

The Duc d'Armand's friend caught her eye—the Englishman. Now what was his name? Dashwood? Yes, that was it. George Dashwood. He was rather tall and gangly, unfashionably clean-shaven, with the milky complexion of someone who spent little time outside. Cece liked those types. Even the arrogant ones mostly managed to hide their disdain beneath a veil of politeness, and the younger they were, the less likely they were to ask for something distasteful. Besides, they had soft hands, and anyone who'd been fingered by a rough-skinned laborer knew that was nothing to be sniffed at. So, while Rossignol mingled with the other guests, she gave the boy a wink, just in case he might be good for a few sous someday.

The boy inclined his head in a bow and made his way over, his hands clasped behind his back. "What a pleasure to see you again, Mademoiselle."

"Enchanted." Cece offered her hand in the delicate way that had become almost second nature to her now, and George hesitated before he bent to kiss it. Just for a fraction of a second, but long enough to make Cece like him more. He was shy of her, and she rather enjoyed it.

"You'll be back at school by the end of the summer, I suppose," she said.

George dropped her hand. "No," he replied, a little too quickly. "I'm finished with all that. I mean to spend the summer painting, then I shall have an exhibition in a gallery come the autumn."

"Oh, how wonderful." Cece beamed. "I adore artists." Then, feeling that he needed a little encouragement, she reached out and ran a finger along his jawline. "You must paint me someday, I think."

"I—I would like nothing more, Mademoiselle." It was sweet, the way his eyes lit up. Sweet enough that Cece's cheeks glowed with warmth. He was handsome, in his own way, and not as adept at hiding his enthusiasm as most men were.

"Then we will make arrangements," she said. "Later. Monsieur Rossignol is calling me."

She took a few steps away then, on an impulse, she turned back and planted a quick kiss on the young man's cheek. Before he could react, she flitted away like a bird, smiling to herself. Taking Rosie's arm, she rejoined Rossignol at the top of the room, where a small stage had been prepared in front of a few rows of seats.

"Are you ready, Mademoiselle Dulac?"

Without waiting for a reply, Rossignol ushered Cece and Rosie onto the stage. The eyes of the assembled partygoers followed the three of them, and the string quartet fell silent. Cece saw herself reflected over and over in the mirrors, but the fine lady in her silk dress seemed like a stranger to the girl from the market town.

"Ladies and gentlemen!" Monsieur Rossignol began. "Some of you I recognize from previous parties. Some of you are new here. To those who are not familiar with my… style of entertainment, let me suggest that if you are of a delicate disposition, you may wish to leave now."

He paused. Nobody moved.

"Very well." Rossignol lowered his voice. "Please, take your seats."

The air was taut with anticipation as the audience settled themselves and their chatter faded. Cece shivered, goosebumps appearing over her bare arms. She glanced at Rosie.

"Is it cold in here?"

"Do you never cease complaining?" Rosie hissed back.

Cece rolled her eyes and turned to smile at her audience. Being the object of such attention made her feel so much more alive. More real. It was as though she only truly existed when she was on stage. But this was different from performing at the Palais. For one thing, she had no idea what was expected of her. And for another, the atmosphere was altogether darker. More intense. Those in the know were expecting something, and the creeping sensation that ran up the back of Cece's neck told her it was something more than a simple song-and-dance number. She glanced at Rosie, but her friend looked perfectly at ease. She was used to this—whatever *this* was.

Rossignol strode across the stage, cane in hand, and stood directly in front of the girls.

"Tonight, ladies and gentlemen, I will show you something that will shock, surprise, and baffle you. Something that defies science and rational thought. Tonight, I mean to prove to you that the dead walk among us, unseen by our eyes. I will prove that ghosts and spirits really do exist, and not only that! They are capable of interacting with us. They have the power to possess our fragile bodies and," he lowered his voice, forcing the audience to hold their collective breath in order to make out his words, "they are hungry for the pleasures of the living. Dim the lights, please, and let the show begin!"

CHAPTER FIVE

"First"—Monsieur Rossignol took hold of Rosie's shoulders and turned her to face him—"we must induce a state of trance in my two beautiful assistants. This will help them become receptive to the influence of the spirits. Look into my eyes, Rosie, and listen only to my voice. I want you to block out all outside distractions, do you understand? There is nobody in this room but you and me."

As he spoke in a soft, monotonous drone, Rosie's features softened; her eyes grew distant and unfocused. Her mouth fell slack, pink lips slightly parted.

"Rosie, when I finish speaking you will respond only to my command, do you understand?"

She answered like a talking doll, without expression. "Yes, Monsieur."

"You will be open to the influence of the spirits, your body a vessel for their use. You have no will of your own, do you understand?"

"Yes, Monsieur."

A new flurry of nerves shuddered through Cece at the sight of Rosie's blank, emotionless face. She imagined herself an empty shell, waiting to be filled, and the thought almost made her bolt off the stage.

She took a deep breath. *It's nothing but a play.* Rosie was acting the part of the marionette to Rossignol's puppet master, that was all. It was no different from the way the dancers moved to the calls of the choreographer during rehearsals.

"No doubt some of you remain skeptical," Rossignol went on, as though he had read Cece's thoughts. "Let me persuade you that Rosie is truly under my power. Rosie, hold out your arm."

Rosie did as she was bid, stretching out one brown limb, palm up, so the softest part of her skin was exposed. Rossignol reached into his pocket, withdrawing a cigar and a book of matches. He lit the cigar and took a slow puff, making no effort to hurry himself. Rosie stood motionless, staring straight ahead.

"Rosie," Rossignol said, "when this cigar touches your skin, you will feel no pain, do you understand?"

"Yes, Monsieur."

There was a sharp intake of breath from the audience as he brought the burning end of the cigar down onto Rosie's arm and held it there for one, two, three seconds. Some women cried out in horrified sympathy. A gentleman objected loudly, but Rossignol ignored him. Cece's heart raced. Suddenly the scars made sense. She could almost feel the burn herself, a fiery tingle spreading out from her heart, as though he had placed the smoldering ash right in the center of her breast. Rosie, though, did not flinch—not even a blink.

Rossignol withdrew the cigar, exposing a furious red welt, and turned the motionless Rosie to face the crowd once more. He closed his eyes and took a long drag on his cigar. In the dim gaslight, shadows cut deep across his face. One of the women in the audience had fainted, and was being helped out by two men, but the others had settled, their flurry of concern for Rosie muted by the desire to know what would happen next. Shrouded in darkness, they seemed little more than a mass of silent, watching eyes.

"I can sense the spirits in this room," Rossignol said, in a hushed voice. "Many of them. They cling to our living bodies with desperate fingers. They want to live again. They want to move. Breathe. *Feel.* Who are we to deny them such pleasure, one last time? Spirits! I give you this body, the body of Rosie Fournier, for your use this night. One of you may enter her, do as you will with her, for this night alone. Which of you will take Rosie?"

There was a long pause. Rossignol's eyes roved the room: watching, waiting. For a moment, Cece thought it would not work. There were no spirits—not really. She herself had been a medium's assistant, working with her mother to fool the old widows in the market square, and she knew as well as anyone that spiritualism was all performance. Fakery. Perhaps Rosie had told Rossignol about Cece's psychic past, and he had chosen her to join in because he knew she would catch on quickly.

26

Then Rosie gasped. She threw her head back, grasping at her heaving chest as though in pain. Moaning, she dropped to her hands and knees, rocking back and forth like an animal. All was rapt silence as she let out one last howl and collapsed into a heap. Cece rushed to her side, but Rossignol warned her away with a glance.

The lights dimmed still further.

Rossignol crouched beside Rosie's crumpled figure and laid a hand on her back. After a long moment of stillness, she lifted her head. Her eyes were wide, the whites clearly showing around her dark irises. A few strands of hair had slipped from her chignon and hung loose around her face. Her lips pulled back in a snarl.

"Stand up," Rossignol said.

Rosie got to her feet. She looked… different. A sheen of sweat covered her skin. Her cheeks glowed. This could not possibly be acting.

"How do you feel?" Rossignol asked.

Rosie's chest heaved with each sharp breath. "Alive." Her voice sounded strange. Deeper than normal.

"And who are you?"

Rosie looked down at herself. "My name is Julia Travers. I died in 1809." She placed her hands on her chest, moving them down over her breasts, her bodice, to her hips.

"Nearly seventy years dead," said Rossignol. "How you must hunger for life."

"I do." Rosie didn't look up from her examination of her own body. She ran her fingers over the scarred skin of her arms, lingering a moment to press their tips to the burn left by the cigar. In her gasp of pain, Cece thought she detected an undertone of pleasure, too.

"This dress…" Rosie pressed her palms to her waist, where her corset was tightest. "So restrictive."

"Cecile, perhaps you could help unlace the dress," Rossignol suggested. "Make Julia more comfortable."

Only then did Rosie seem to notice Cece for the first time, eyeing her ravenously. Cece had the unnerving feeling it was not Rosie looking at her, but the spirit, seeing through Rosie's eyes. Nervously, she moved behind her and unhooked the buttons on the back of the dress to reach the corset within. *It's just acting.* She fumbled with the ribbons. *Just a performance, like any other.* But her palms were damp, and the satin slipped from her fingers every time Rosie breathed.

It wasn't as though Cece had never made an exhibition of herself with another woman before. There were rich men who liked to pay for two or even three girls to 'perform' at small gatherings—birthday parties usually—but those events had been about good-natured, bawdy fun. This was different. The audience was bigger, and full of unfamiliar people. The tension in the air was stretched tight as a rubber band, ready to snap.

Rosie let out a sigh of relief as the tight bones of the corset loosened.

"Thank God," she declared. "I felt I was being squeezed in a vice. This body is"—she pushed the sleeves of her dress down to reveal an expanse of bare shoulder—"delightful." She wriggled her shoulders, and the pink silk slid over her body to pool at her feet, leaving Rosie in her white shift and petticoats. A few boys in the audience whooped at the sight. Rossignol turned to them.

"Perhaps, ladies and gentlemen, it is time we let another spirit through into our corporeal world. Cecile, are you ready?"

Cece looked out at the audience, sensing their anticipation. They wanted this. Whatever they were here to see, they needed it. A release. A chance to let go of their daily cares. It was what they came to the theatre for, but this was something different. Something more.

Glancing at the front row, she saw George Dashwood watching, and something about his expression—confused but full of longing—sent a thrill through her. How he wanted her. How they all wanted her. She took a deep breath.

"I'm ready."

"Then look into my eyes, and listen only to my voice."

Rossignol's eyes were the blue-green of calm water, his voice as gentle as a summer breeze. As he spoke, a warm glow flooded Cece's body. Her muscles relaxed. The audience, the stage, even George—all were forgotten, and she felt perfectly calm and supported, as though she were lying in a soft feather bed. Finally, even his voice blurred, fading in and out as she drifted in a daze.

"Spirits! I give you this body, the body of Cecile Dulac, for your use this night. One of you may enter her, do as you will with her, for this night alone. Which of you will take Cecile?"

A tingle began at the tips of Cece's fingers and toes. It crept up her limbs like spreading flame, setting her skin on fire. When it hit her torso, her chest clenched. She couldn't breathe. Something was crawling inside her, filling her up, settling into the nooks and crevasses of her body. And it burned—burned with a thrill of violent desire. The room shot back into full clarity: the lights brighter, the sounds stronger, the colors more vivid than ever before.

She turned her head from side to side, experiencing it all as if for the first time. The cheering of the crowd surged into her ears like a wave breaking on the beach. The gaslights flared, casting their feverish glow over every face. In the mirrors, a thousand eyes watched. Blood pulsed through her veins, warm and vital, and when she caught sight of her face in the mirror, she saw the same bright spark in her eyes that she had seen in Rosie's.

"Who are you?" Rossignol asked, an edge of eagerness in his voice.

"Selena," she heard herself say, from a distance, in a voice unlike her own.

"Selena." He spoke the name almost tenderly, his eyes never straying from hers, as though he were searching for something hidden inside her. "How did you die?"

"I drowned myself." A murmur of shock ran through the audience. Anger gripped Cece's heart—fury so strong she could tear everyone in the room to shreds and still not have spent it. "My husband drove me to it. I had no choice!"

"You desire revenge," said Rossignol.

"Yes." Cece's gaze roved over the audience, picking out every male face. She hated them all. She wanted them to suffer. Every last one of them.

"And you shall have it. Another time."

For a moment, Selena's rage turned on Rossignol, but it could not sustain. At the sight of him it withered and died away, leaving nothing but a hollow ache—a sadness more frightening to Cece than the anger had been. Rossignol took her hand in one of his, Rosie's in the other.

"Look where you are, Selena. Think about what you might do, while you walk on this Earth again." He smiled. "How beautiful you both are."

What I might do… Cece gazed at Rosie. How beautiful she was, indeed. Beneath her thin shift, her rose-colored nipples were faintly visible. Cece had never looked at a woman in that way, but now that she did, it was all she could see. At the thought of running her hands over that skin—of kissing that perfectly curved neck—a warm ache spread between her legs. At that moment, she wanted Rosie more than she had ever wanted anything before.

Rossignol moved behind her and she felt his fingers at her back, untying the laces of her dress. As it dropped to the floor, Rosie took a step towards her. She ran a hand over Cece's cheek, looking deep into her eyes, then let the tip of her thumb graze her lips. Without thinking, Cece opened her mouth slightly, and let Rosie's thumb slip inside, sucking on it, her eyes never leaving her friend's. Rosie withdrew her thumb and their lips met in a kiss—tentative at first, then growing deeper as passion consumed them.

Intoxicated by Rosie's sweet taste, Cece let her tongue gently probe her friend's mouth, sliding her hands down to her waist. As they drew closer, their breasts pressed against each other, nipples hardening. The goading calls of the audience were mere echoes to Cece—a ringing in her ears. She was dimly aware of Rossignol's hands on her shoulders, sliding the sleeves of her shift down over her arms.

Rosie pulled away from the kiss and helped him pull Cece's shift down to her waist, exposing her breasts. She ran a line of kisses down Cece's neck, over her collarbones. Tracing her way down to one nipple, she swirled her tongue over it, sending sparks through her body.

Cece sighed, knotting her fingers in Rosie's dark hair, unravelling it from its chignon until it fell around her shoulders. Then, she guided Rosie's mouth over to her other breast, reveling in the pleasure of it, trying to stave off the growing need between her legs just a little longer. She was alive. *Alive.* Risen from the depths and hungry for lust, for life, and for revenge.

CHAPTER SIX

"Is this what you brought me here for?" George glanced sidelong at Bastian.

Bastian kept his eyes fixed on the stage. "You seemed to like the look of Cecile. I thought you would surely enjoy this."

In the semi-darkness, the two women were little more than silhouettes, the dim light tracing their curves. The line of Cecile's back, slightly arched. The halo of Rosie's curly hair as she kissed her way down Cecile's stomach. And behind them, Rossignol, presiding over the two of them like a proud father.

George clenched his fists until his nails dug into his palms. *Any other girl.* Any other girl, and he would have been riveted to the scene just as Bastian was. What difference did it make, after all? They were only whores, and this spiritualist nonsense was no more than an excuse to have them undress for an audience. The pleasures of the living, indeed!

But this girl. *This girl.* For all her earthly charm, George had been convinced there was something different about her—something that ought to have made her rise above a degenerate display such as this. A look in her eyes, perhaps. A certain sweetness about her smile. He had imagined her sitting by his hearth, back in England, the very picture of a lady. For one crazed moment, when he'd offered to paint her, he'd considered that maybe, just maybe…

But no. How could he even consider taking such a woman back to England? To his father? The scandal would be unthinkable.

Rosie pushed Cecile's petticoats down her hips, and Cecile curled her fingers in her friend's hair. Rosie knelt, moving her head between Cecile's legs, gripping her shapely hips with both hands. In the rapt silence, every exhale of Cecile's, however soft, carried straight to George's ears as if she sighed for him alone. His hardness pressed uncomfortably against the fabric of his trousers. It was torture. He ought to leave. He wanted to leave.

Instead, he found himself leaning forward, wishing that he could somehow pierce the thick cloak of darkness that shrouded the two women, to see a little more beyond the hints of flesh that were all he could make out. He had studied the female form before, in the bright, clinical daylight of an artist's studio, but this was different. The seeing and yet not seeing. The tantalizing glimpses.

Rossignol stood behind Cecile, placing his hands on her shoulders, sliding his hands down to cup her breasts. George loathed him. How could he? How could *she*? But she was so beautiful it made him ache, and he could not look away.

Cecile let out a little cry. George peered closer. Rossignol had one of her nipples between his thumb and forefinger, pinching it.

"Consider, my ladies and gentlemen," he said, in a husky voice, "how starved these spirits have been. Lost for so long in the eternal darkness of death. Wandering, cold and alone, yearning for a warm touch. Pleasure and pain are all the same to them. It is feeling that they crave."

Cecile gasped again, her breathing ragged. Rossignol let go of her and instead gripped Rosie's hair, pulling her up until she was forced to stand. Cecile moaned in disappointment, running her hands over her breasts, her stomach, to the dark curl of hair below. When she tried to slip a finger between her legs, Rossignol took hold of her wrists and held them firmly behind her.

She struggled, twisting, trying to reach her captor's face with her lips, and George began to believe, for the first time, in the possibility that she was truly possessed. She moaned like a wild creature, focused on nothing but sating her desires.

"Please, Alexandre," she purred, her chest heaving. "More. I need… more."

George's surprise at hearing her refer to Rossignol by his Christian name was washed away in the moment, as the puppet master beckoned to Rosie.

"Hold her," he directed, and Rosie took over the task of securing Cecile's arms, calming her by nuzzling at her neck. Cecile turned to meet her lips, and the two women melted into a kiss. A few of the men in the audience cheered, and Rossignol chucked indulgently.

"You think my intention is only to titillate," he said, as he pulled the pins from Cecile's hair so it fell in golden waves around her shoulders. All she now wore was a choker necklace set with a ruby. "I can assure you, that is not the case."

George tore his eyes away from Cecile and glanced at the crowd. Nobody seemed to care what their host's intention might be. The gentlemen were content to gorge their eyes on the display in front of them. The women were all dancers, actresses, chorus girls, poised to take advantage of the men's excitement to earn themselves a little money later in the evening. A shudder of disgust ran through him. They could dress as ladies, even affect the insouciance of an elite Parisienne, but that was all a veneer. A performance. Perhaps all Rossignol had done was scrub off the veneer, to show Cecile for what she really was. Titillation was what they were all there for, so why the pretense?

But Rossignol was keen to have his say.

"I want to prove to you," he went on, "that this is no mere show. I want you to walk away from here tonight believing that the dead can be reborn; that spirits can walk among us; and that, what is more, they can remain. All they require is a willing vessel, and the right treatment. What you are watching is not simply a performance, but an experiment. One that you are all a vital part of."

Rossignol withdrew a skein of silk from his pocket and bound Cecile's hands. A servant passed an object up to him—a wooden paddle, rather like a large hairbrush. George stiffened, torn between his impulse to intervene and helpless fascination.

"This is wrong," he muttered to Bastian.

"Relax, Georgie!" Bastian grinned. "Enjoy yourself." Without taking his eyes off Cecile, he reached for the whore to his right, pulling her into a kiss, then pushing her head down between his legs, where she crouched, fumbling tipsily with the buttons of his trousers.

"Selena." Rossignol ran the backs of his fingers over Cecile's cheek, almost tenderly. "How does it feel to return to the land of the living?"

Cecile sighed, her eyelids flickering. "There's so much... so much to feel. Don't make me go back." She moaned as Rosie dropped to her knees once more and resumed her ministrations. "I don't want to go back... there."

"What was it like there, Selena?" Rossignol ran the paddle slowly down the length of her back, bringing it to rest just above the curve of her behind.

"Dark. So dark. And cold. I was numb. There was nothing. Oh!"

She squealed. Rossignol had drawn his hand back and slapped her. Her eyes flew open wide.

"Nothing?" he asked. "No pleasure? No... pain?"

"No." Cecile's cheeks flushed bright pink. "Nothing." She shot him a look that seemed equal parts fear and excitement, and he hit her again. This time her cry was closer to a moan. George's blood surged, his cheeks growing hot with fury. He pictured himself storming up to the stage, demanding that Rossignol release Cecile. Taking her away with him, and... and...

"Again?" Rossignol asked.

"Again. Please."

"Good God." Bastian had his hands on his whore's head, pushing her back down every time she tried to come up for air. "I'd heard stories about these parties, but this is—" He broke off as Rossignol aimed a third swipe at Cecile. The future Duc d'Armand wasn't the only one who had dispensed with all pretense of civility—much of the audience were doing similarly, under cover of darkness.

George glanced at the whore, her lips wrapped around Bastian's tumescence, burying him deep. How would it feel...? His hand drifted to his crotch, and the pleasure that shot through him as his palm made contact made him stifle a gasp. He was rubbing himself through his trousers before he even realized what he was doing. He couldn't stop. He wanted more. He wanted Cecile. To be inside her. To feel her tightness swallow him. To hurt her.

This last thought shocked George back to his senses, and his stomach swam with disgust. At Rossignol, at Bastian and the rest of the audience, but most of all at himself. Fearing he would be sick, he got to his feet and tore himself away from the sight of Cecile, now bent over, with Rossignol holding her up by her hair. He hurried from the room, leaving the shouts and exuberance behind him, and out of the nearest door, into the cool night air.

Finding himself in a garden, he stood doubled over for a moment, retching. But he did not vomit, and once he had recovered himself, his heart pounded and his blood rushed worse than ever. Unlacing his trousers, he jerked himself to a quick, explosive orgasm, then stood there as the rush faded, feeling empty as a hollow shell.

CHAPTER SEVEN

Cece woke groggily, from a sleep so deep and dreamless she might have been dead. She lay in a soft feather bed, bright sunlight streaming through the curtains. A loud snore made her jump, and she looked around to find Rosie curled up naked beside her, sheets tangled around her legs.

Cece tried to roll over, but every muscle in her body ached. Slowly, she pushed herself up, wincing at the twinges that accompanied her every movement. Her arms were covered in red marks. Her torso was the same. Prodding at them brought tears to her eyes.

On a nearby chair hung her dress, messily discarded. She slipped out of bed and put it on, examining her surroundings. It was a fine room, richly furnished with a large oak wardrobe and plush carpets: she was surely still in Chateau Rossignol. She remembered arriving, being led on stage... And then her memories became blurred and uncertain. She dimly recalled Rosie's transformation, but after that—nothing.

What happened to her? Where did all these bruises come from?

She finished dressing and turned to the nearest mirror. On the table beneath it lay her hairpins and the ruby choker. She pinned her hair up as best she could, then reached for the necklace, looking into the mirror as she held it against her throat.

Don't make me go back. I don't want to go back... there.

The thought tumbled into Cece's mind as if from nowhere. It was as clear and sharp as a blade, and it was not hers. The face in the mirror flickered, its lips curling into a cruel smile. Cece tied the black ribbon around her throat with trembling fingers. Then, leaving Rosie to sleep, she hurried downstairs.

Finding the house silent, she slipped out of a back entrance into Rossignol's vast garden. Hoping to find a gate from which she could leave unnoticed, she struck out down the nearest path, reassuring herself that the high hedges would hide her from the sight of anyone looking out of a window. As she walked, the paths twisted and turned, folding back on themselves, now and then running into dead ends. After a few minutes wandering, she was forced to admit she was hopelessly lost. When she tried to retrace her steps, she found that she could not.

Heart racing, she picked up her pace, walking faster and faster until she broke into a run. Just when she thought the maze would never end, she flew out from between the hedges into a clearing. There, beneath the clear blue sky, lay a lake—round and still and shining in the sun. A sudden horror seized Cece at the sight of it: her chest contracted, and for a moment all she could see in her mind's eye was watery blackness. It was as though the lake was forcing itself down her throat, squeezing the air from her lungs. She looked into the water and her reflection distorted. For a blink of an eye, she thought she saw someone else looking up at her from the depths. Green eyes, dark hair, one pale hand reaching up to the surface. Reaching for her.

Startled, Cece turned and ran, not caring which way she went.

It took her only a few moments to find the gate. She had the strangest sensation that, having shown her what it wanted her to see, the garden was now allowing her to leave. She fumbled with the latch, panic still fluttering in her chest, and flung herself out onto the busy street.

CHAPTER EIGHT

"I'm here to see Mademoiselle Dulac. I was told this is her address."

The maid who'd answered the door frowned up at George. She couldn't have been much older than twelve, but her expression put him in mind of a world-weary old woman.

"She's indisposed," the girl said, flatly.

"Perhaps I could wait?"

"If you must." She stepped aside, and George entered the musty-smelling hallway. The boarding house had the air of a place made to look grand on as small a budget as possible. The fixtures and fittings had been slathered with gold paint, and the carpets, though thick, were threadbare and ill-fitting. Here and there the wallpaper bulged, and the stench of damp permeated everything.

The maid led George into an empty reception room and left without a word. He was about to sit on one of the sofas when he noticed a large stain on the cushion. Instead, he remained standing, and walked to the window to look out onto the narrow lane below.

He hadn't been able to stop replaying the previous night's events in his mind. That he'd failed to step in and prevent the debauchery lay heavily on his conscience. Not only had he sat and watched while Cecile was so defiled, he had even, in some way, enjoyed it. The thought made his skin crawl. As a man of honor, it was incumbent on him to make amends to Cecile. However low she may have sunk in his estimation, he had gone to the party with the intention of keeping her safe, and he had failed.

Over the course of the day, his promise to paint her had returned to his mind. Perhaps some donation to her living expenses might help recompense her for what she had suffered at Rossignol's hands. His father could hardly criticize him for hiring a model for his artwork, after all.

He waited for some time, watching a group of urchins playing in the alleyway, but as the sun dipped behind the rooftops, there was no sign of Cecile. He returned to the hallway and called for the maid, but nobody answered. It seemed clear that Cecile was not interested in seeing him—or perhaps the maid simply hadn't bothered to pass on his message. Either way, he had given up and was shrugging on his coat when he heard a door open and a soft footstep.

"You wanted to see me?"

Cecile wore a simple, loose-fitting gown, open at the front to reveal a white nightdress. Her hair hung loose around her shoulders, and her eyes were rimmed with dark circles. Around her neck was the same ruby she'd worn the night before. She looked exhausted, but she retained a knowing air as she wandered over to a nearby cabinet, glancing over her shoulder with a slight smile before taking out two smudged glasses.

"Perhaps I can get you a drink, Monsieur…?"

"Dashwood," George reminded her.

"Monsieur Dashwood. To what do I owe the pleasure of your company?"

"I wanted to know if there was anything I could do to help you, after…"

He trailed off, unsure how to continue. Cecile remained silent, pouring two glasses of red wine. She handed one to him, and took a sip from the other.

"Please, do sit down."

As she spoke, her voice wavered, and a look of confusion passed across her face.

"You are not well, Mademoiselle," George burst out. "Let me help you." He took her hand to steady her and helped her sink onto the sofa. "Please, tell me what afflicts you. Is there anything I can do?"

"You're a sweet boy." She smiled. "I'm perfectly well. But perhaps," she moved a little closer to him, "there's something I can do for you?"

"No. No, I don't want to—I mean, I didn't intend—I mean…" George looked down. "Mademoiselle, I apologize if my appearance here this evening has implied something untoward. I ought to leave."

He was about to stand, but Cecile took his arm. "Stay. You were there last night. Can you tell me…" Here, she looked up at him with her blue eyes, her face a picture of perfect innocence. "Can you tell me what happened?"

George's face grew hot. "You don't recall?"

Cecile shook her head. "I remember very little. Something came over me. I couldn't control it. I was not myself."

She looked so fragile that George had an urge to take her up in his arms and reassure her everything would be all right. But how could he? He didn't even know what Rossignol had done to her after he'd left.

"You must not go back there," he insisted. "It's not safe. Promise me. Promise you won't go back."

"Monsieur Dashwood…" Cecile smiled faintly.

He shook his head. "Call me George, please."

"George." Her hand drifted to her ruby. "I'm afraid I… I'm not sure I have a choice. All day I've been feeling so very strange. I shall go back, I feel sure of it. I feel… compelled."

George gripped her hand. "He hypnotized you! You must still be under his power. How can I help you? I must do something."

"I am frightened of him—of Rossignol—but, George, would you think less of me if I admitted I don't want you to do anything? I feel different today, but not unwell. Better, I suppose, in a way. Stronger. More alive. I ache all over, but I don't mind the pain. Besides, there's the money to think of."

"I'm sure there are plenty of men who would die to be your patron. You mustn't feel you have to do… what you did last night."

Cecile placed a delicate hand on his thigh. "Are you offering?"

"I doubt I could afford you, on the stipend my father gives me."

Her fingers kneaded his thigh. "I'm sure you could find the money from somewhere… if you wanted it enough."

"Let me paint you instead. I only need a day or two to arrange a studio, and—"

Cecile waved his suggestion away. Her gaze strayed to his abandoned satchel. "You have your drawing things with you, I see?"

"I have."

"Well." She lounged back on the sofa. "Perhaps we ought to start now?"

"Now?" George took a sip of wine to soothe his dry throat. "Well, the light…"

Cecile laughed. "My God! He's worried about the light! I'll fetch some more candles, if that would help?"

"No, no… What we have here is sufficient. How much?"

"Shh! We can discuss payment afterwards." She stood and slipped off her dressing gown. "How do you want me?"

Seeing her hands straying to the buttons of her nightdress, George held up a hand to stop her. Already his heart raced, and he feared she would notice his excitement.

"Really, Mademoiselle, that is not necessary."

"Not necessary? You artists like your models to be nude, do you not?"

"I could draw your face, for now. It's really…"

But Cecile was already half out of her nightdress, and before George could say any more, she stood before him with nothing on but her ruby choker, and he had no further power to argue. Even her willingness to disrobe seemed disconcertingly innocent, as though it were entirely natural and blameless that she should be naked in front of him. Alone. His father would have condemned her. George knew he ought to do likewise, but the sweetness of her smile, combined with her simple trust of him, only made his heart warm to her more.

"Shall I lie down?" she asked, lowering herself onto the sofa. Then, her eyes brightened with a sudden thought, and she got up to fetch a rose from a nearby vase. "A little prop, perhaps, just for interest."

As she settled back against the cushions, she brought the petals to her lips, looking at George over the flower with a glint in her eye. Swallowing hard, he arranged himself in a nearby chair and took out his sketchbook.

Looking at her was like staring directly at the sun. Despite her tired eyes, her radiance glowed from within. Her skin was smooth and golden, the lines of her body soft and inviting. He was aware of her eyes on his face like two hot pinpoints as he studied the roundness of her breasts, the hourglass curve of her hips. Noticing the pink vestiges of scratches on her thighs, his thoughts returned to the night before. Rosie's pink lips on Cecile's nipples. Cecile with her head thrown back, skin glowing with sweat, mouth open in a sigh of ecstasy.

The ruby sparkled in the dying light.

The easiest thing was not to look at her face. Instead, he concentrated on one body part at a time, immersing his attention in the simple shapes; the areas of light and shadow. Cecile was quiet and still and, in time, George regained his focus, despite his persisting excitement. The only sound in the room was the scratch of pencil on paper.

"Have you drawn many women?" she said, after a while.

George laughed, his face burning. "A few."

"Private sittings, like this?"

"No. Just you."

She smiled. "Then I feel special. I thought you artists were worldly men."

"I suppose we all have to start somewhere."

Cecile smiled, and traced the rose over her collarbones. She slid it down her chest, teasing first one nipple then the other.

"Ever since last night, I swear my senses are heightened. I feel so... much. Just
this—" she ran the rose petals down to her navel, "is like heaven."

George put down his pencil. Cecile drew a line with the rose down to the dark triangle between her legs, spreading them slightly apart. Then she paused, looking at George, her chest moving softly with every breath.

"It's as though I died and came back to life," she whispered. "I have this need... I can't help it."

She spread her legs still further, teasing the rose petals over the pink lips barely visible beneath her curls of dark hair. Her hips made tiny thrusts, and with her free hand she reached for a nipple, pinching it between her fingertips. Once more he was reminded of the night before. There was a glassy look in her eyes, as though the puppet master still directed her movements.

"I should go."

It took a superhuman effort just to utter the words, but utter them he did, and he was almost on his feet by the time she replied.

"Mmm, no. Please. Stay."

It was her little sigh that broke him. A sigh that seemed so full of promise; that whispered of hours of delirious pleasure, if only he would leave aside his reservations and take what she offered. And what were his reservations, after all? His mind was so fogged he could hardly remember.

"How much?" he said, hoarsely. "Name your price."

"Come here."

He went to kneel beside her and she ran a hand through his hair, drawing him down so their faces almost touched.

"You're sweet," she said, her mouth so near to his he could almost taste her. "Not like the others."

"No," said George, although he hardly knew what he was agreeing to. "Not like the others."

And then he kissed her, her lips soft and yielding beneath his. Her tongue teased its way into his mouth and he tasted the rich sweetness of red wine. She wrapped her arms around his neck and he ran his hands down her back, marveling at the downy softness of her skin. Breaking away from her kiss, he buried his face in her neck to inhale her warm, powdery scent. Without thinking, he nipped at her shoulder with his teeth. Cecile grabbed his hand and moved it to her breast.

"Hurt me," she whispered.

"I can't do that."

"Do it!" Her voice was husky, insistent. How could he refuse? George pinched her nipple between his fingers and twisted it as hard as he dared. Her cry of mingled pleasure and agony made him shudder. Was it delight, or disgust at himself? Whatever it was, it made him even harder.

Cecile spread her legs, wrapping them around his waist, pulling him close. She kissed his neck, nibbled at his ear, and murmured, "Fuck me. I want you inside me."

George moved back a little, fumbling to unlace his trousers, and looked into her eyes—intense, full of animal need. But behind that was something else—something that made him shrink back. Something more like anger.

And he liked it.

"Fuck me," she insisted again, pulling him into a ravenous kiss. She bit down on his lip, drawing blood, and the taste of metal filled George's mouth. He thrust himself inside her, twisting his hands in her hair as she drew him deeper. She was so soft. So warm. Her body invited him, hugged him, just as he had imagined. His orgasm built, tension tight like a coil.

"Cecile," he murmured.

"Selena," she breathed. "Call... me... Selena."

She arched her back, crying out, and George let go, coming inside her with one final, desperate thrust. Cecile fell back against the cushions, panting, and he withdrew to sit back on his haunches, staring at her. Selena? Had she said Selena? Did it matter? She moaned, still shuddering, and her fingers found the ruby around her neck.

"It's too tight," she said, suddenly. "Too tight."

Her eyes flew open; she sat up, clawing at the black ribbon. "I can't get it off. Help me. Please, help me!"

George reached around her and untied the ribbon. The choker fell into his hand, and Cecile slumped back, eyes closed, fast asleep. Confused and unable to rouse her, George covered her as best he could with her robe, left some money on the table, and went away.

CHAPTER NINE

Cece slept on the sofa through most of the following day. By the time she woke it was mid-afternoon and she'd already missed the rehearsal for that night's show. Cursing the maid for not waking her, she rushed to the theatre and dressed as quickly as she could manage with her aching limbs. Try as she might, she couldn't quite piece together what had happened during George's visit. Her memories were like a series of postcards scattered to the wind: George coming to enquire after her—how sweet he was! Getting his sketchbook out to draw her. The way he'd looked at her, as though she were the only woman in the world.

And then…? Cece frowned, trying to remember through the haze.

"You look like death," said Rosie, as pink-cheeked and pretty as ever.

Cece glanced in the mirror. Perhaps it was the light, but Rosie was right—she looked as drained as she felt. A sudden fear shook her: that her audience would find her faded and dull; that their cheers would not be so loud, or their gifts as generous. Sevigny would take one look at her and decide to drop her as his favorite starlet. The posters with her face on would be brought down, and in their place…

"You can't go on stage like that," Rosie said. Was it just Cece's imagination, or was there a glimmer of triumph in her smile? "You need something to brighten you up. Here, try some rouge."

Cece took the pot and applied it liberally, but the artificial blush did nothing to restore the sparkle that should have been in her eyes. She looked like a doll, blank and featureless, her eyes as expressionless as painted enamel.

"It's no good." She sighed. "Nobody will want to watch me when I look like this." She shivered. "Is it cold in here?"

"I'm as warm as anything." Rosie came up behind her to pin the straps of Cece's dress, attaching the two brooches that held it together. The brush of her fingers on Cece's skin was like fire rushing over ice—intense, and soon extinguished. "What about that necklace Monsieur Rossignol gave you? The ruby brings out the glow in your cheeks. Nobody will mind you wearing it."

"I'm sure I left it at home…" Cece began, but Rosie pointed at the dressing table.

"Of course you didn't. I saw you take it out of your bag when you first got here." She picked it up and held it to Cece's throat. "There now, you look better already. Put it on."

She was right. The ruby had a magical effect on her. The moment she tied the ribbon around her throat, her face brightened, her eyes sparkled, and a rush of life flowed into her body, like blood returning to a deadened limb.

"Beautiful." Rosie slipped a hand around her waist and kissed her on the cheek. "You will have your pick of men by the end of tonight's show."

I will. Cece's reflection shimmered in the mirror. She imagined them all at her feet, begging for her favors. *I will have them all, and they will all pay.*

She turned away to head for the stage, blazing inwardly, now certain she would put on the performance of a lifetime. But before she left the dressing room, she caught a last glimpse in the mirror that shot her through with an icicle of fear. Her reflection was sinking into watery blackness. Her face was grey, corpse like. A red-tinged darkness settled over her vision.

Cece leant against the doorframe, breathing deeply until the vision dissipated and the room snapped back to life. The lights blazed harder than ever, and a stagehand's voice echoed from the hallway, shouting the final call. Collecting herself, she hurried to the wings.

There, she stood behind the curtain, listening to the buzz of the audience. Her skin tingled: they were all there to see her. A rush of excitement seized her, and by the time the curtain rose and she darted onto the stage, she felt she held the world in her hands. She swayed under the hot stage lights, at first following the steps she'd been taught. Then, as her limbs grew warmer and the adulation of the audience flowed through her veins like honey, she added her own little flourishes. A wriggle of the hips here; a tantalizing pose there. Riveted faces and wide eyes filled the front row, transfixed by her. She could have destroyed any one of them with a single glance.

Struck by a sudden impulse, Cece slipped behind one of the silken drapes that hung from the rafters, and unpinned the broaches holding her straps, letting the dress flow off her shoulders like water. As the music ended, she struck a pose, naked, hidden only by the thin curtain of silk. Rapturous applause swept the theatre, and she basked in it.

When she left the theatre at the end of the show, her arms brimming with bouquets, she found Rossignol waiting at the stage door.

"You were beautiful." He kissed her on the cheek. "Perfection. Allow me to carry some of these."

He took a bunch of red roses and plucked out the card.

"I see the Comte has not given up his attempts to earn your favor."

Cece laughed. "He won't succeed. Not a bore like him. Not when I have you," she added, suddenly strangely certain that she did have him. Although she barely knew him, and he was by far her superior in terms of rank and fortune, it seemed altogether natural that he should belong to her entirely. *You are mine. Body and soul.* Words whispered in darkness. Cece's mind flooded with memories that couldn't possibly have been hers: lovemaking by firelight; his lips on her neck, his hands gripping her hips. *Alexandre.*

"But perhaps Sevigny *should* succeed." Rossignol's voice brought her back to the moment, as he showed her to his carriage. "He is throwing a ball tomorrow night. I suggest you attend, as my guest, and allow him a little of your time."

Cece stopped, looking at him over a cascade of lilies. "Why, whatever for?"

"For me, my dear." He took the rest of the flowers and piled them into the carriage, before helping her to climb in herself. Once they set off, he continued: "The Comte is a despicable fellow. A liar, a drunkard, and a gambler. He drove his own wife to kill herself. Did you know that?"

Cece studied Rossignol's grave expression. "Forgive me, but why would you want me to spend time with a man like that? The very thought makes me shudder."

Rossignol leaned forward, fixing her with his sea-green gaze. "I'm sure it does. Doesn't the idea of him disgust you? His flabby flesh? His sweaty hands all over your body? Wouldn't you like to punish him for what he did?"

Cece's mind floated on the soft lilt of his voice. The rattle of the carriage and the clatter of the horses' hooves died away, and all that remained were Rossignol's words. She could picture the scene: the distraught wife; the violent, drunken husband. The desperation that must have led her to kill herself…

And then she was sinking. Drowning, black water closing above her head as the world grew more and more distant. Hatred swallowed her whole, and when she looked at Rossignol again, she felt a wave of pure fury wash over her. *You left me. I needed you, and you left me.*

"Spend a little time with him." Rossignol pushed something cold and hard into her hand. A dagger. "Punish him. Will you do that, Selena?"

"Yes, Monsieur," Cece heard herself say. "I will."

CHAPTER TEN

The whole of Paris knew the Comte du Sevigny threw a ball like no other. That night's gathering, in the Comte's chateau just outside the city, was a masquerade themed around the Roman festival of Saturnalia, thrown for the Comte's birthday. The Lord of Misrule, the invitations explained, would preside over an evening of debauchery, and all must do as he directed, on pain of death.

Knowing all the ladies of Paris would be there, decked in their finest frills and flounces, Cece decided to cut as striking a figure as possible. She wanted every head turned in her direction—especially that of the Comte himself. With the help of Monsieur Rossignol, she procured a costume she was sure would guarantee her the attention she craved. A simple, flowing gown in pure white, draped to show off her figure. Her hair was curled in delicate ringlets, and her only jewelry was the ruby choker. Tucked into a garter accessible through a slit in her gown was the dagger Rossignol had given her, matching rubies glinting in its hilt.

"Do me proud, my dear Selena," he whispered, as they ascended the steps of Sevigny's chateau.

Fiery torches burned on either side of the open doorway, and from inside echoed raucous laughter. The Lord of Misrule was already making the most of his birthday celebrations, and as Rossignol and Cece entered he was careening drunkenly around the ballroom in his Satyr costume, groping at any ladies unlucky enough to pass him by. Around the room stood gold-painted human 'statues' in various states of undress. Servants wove between the guests, carrying jugs of red wine and trays overflowing with exotic fruit.

Seeing Rossignol, Sevigny blundered over to shake his hand. The Comte wore papier-mâché goat horns on either side of his head, and brown trousers made of horsehair. A thin linen shirt barely covered the expanse of his belly. Beady black eyes regarded Rossignol with thinly veiled dislike.

"A surprise to see you here, old friend! What a pleasure. And with my little ingénue on your arm, too." He kissed Cece on both cheeks, leaning in to mutter, "I heard you made quite the sensation at the Palais last night with your little… improvisation, Mademoiselle. A shame I wasn't there to see it."

Cece curtsied, forcing herself not to back away from his overpowering smell of sweat and wine. "I hope you approve, sir."

"Approve?! Ticket sales are booming, my dear. There hasn't been a dancer more popular since my wife was alive."

As he spoke of his wife, he glanced at Rossignol, his eyes hardening.

"Perhaps I might take little Cecile off your hands for a while, Monsieur," he said. "You do the rest of us a terrible disservice by keeping her all to yourself."

Rossignol took a step back. "Please, be my guest. I'm sure Mademoiselle Dulac would be honored to accompany you."

Cece didn't need to force a smile. The thought of destroying this piece of human filth gave her a powerful thrill, and as Sevigny led her onto the dancefloor, her delight was unfeigned.

The string quartet struck up a waltz; Sevigny slid his hand around Cece's waist, his fingers hot through the thin fabric of her dress. In his drunken state, he struggled to keep up with the steps, so Cece led him as best she could, steering him away from the other couples and into a quieter corner. He pulled her closer, and his erection pressed against her thigh.

"What a beauty," he murmured, not bothering to dance any longer, his hands roving over her back.

"My lord, people are watching us."

Sevigny laughed. "What do you care, my pretty whore? Are you worried about your reputation? Everyone heard what you did at Rossignol's the other night."

Anger rose in Cece's chest, a fiery blaze, so strong she was sure he would feel its heat. But she quelled it as best she could and put a finger to his lips.

"I only mean, my lord, that perhaps we ought to go somewhere more private."

Sevigny hesitated, his eyes narrowing. Did he think he might persuade her into a repeat performance of whatever had happened at Rossignol's? She still didn't know the details of the night, but she'd heard the whispers, seen the way the other girls looked at her in the dressing room, with a mixture of envy and disdain. She had a reputation, that was for certain, but it was not the one she wanted. She didn't want to be looked at the way Sevigny was looking at her, as though she was barely worthy to polish his cock. She wanted to be admired. Respected. Feared.

And by the end of tonight, she would be.

CHAPTER ELEVEN

Selena.

The name echoed around George's mind as he and Bastian headed into the ballroom. Bastian, as a member of the French aristocracy, had naturally been invited to the Comte's party, and George had been quick to accept the opportunity to join him, hoping to catch a glimpse of Cecile.

Call me Selena, she'd said, as she gripped him in the throes of passion. What had she meant by that? Selena was the name of the ghost Rossignol had invited to possess her—but surely that was all fabrication? Had the ordeal she'd endured somehow affected Cecile? The only way he could reassure himself was to seek her out again, and the ball was the obvious opportunity.

The Comte's high-society party was an altogether different sort of affair to Rossignol's illicit gathering, at least on the surface. Bastian introduced George to a posse of boisterous young nobles, and they drank and caroused, and watched Sevigny make himself increasingly foolish with one lady after another. Several of the gentlemen had been guests at Rossignol's, however, and when the conversation inevitably turned to Cecile—*she was delectable! The most exquisite female they'd ever laid eyes upon!*—George hastily attempted to change the subject by enquiring why Rossignol was absent from the Comte's ball.

"Why, Rossignol and Sevigny are sworn enemies," Bastian said, as though the fact were so obvious George ought to have known it somehow. "I dare say we won't be seeing him tonight."

"Enemies? Why?"

"They used to run the Palais together," said one of Bastian's companions, a foppish boy with long hair. "Until Sevigny cheated Rossignol out of a vast sum during an evening's gambling."

"Not so, not so!" protested another, taking a swig of wine. "It was Rossignol who cheated the Comte."

"Nonsense," Bastian cut in. "My father told me it had something to do with Sevigny's wife. The Comtesse used to be a dancer herself, you know."

"So I heard." The fop raised his eyebrows. "Quite the scandal when she drowned herself. I'm sure Rossignol's name was mentioned in connection with it all."

"Hold on." George nudged his friend. "You were saying?"

Standing in the doorway was Rossignol himself, dressed as the Emperor Caesar, with none other than Cecile Dulac on his arm.

"Well, I never." Bastian laughed, as Sevigny approached the new arrivals. "This could be interesting."

But there was no trouble to be seen. Instead, after a short negotiation, Rossignol handed Cecile over to the Comte, and the two of them soon disappeared through a discreet side-door.

Leaving Bastian with his friends, George slipped away to follow them.

Out in the silent hallway, he spotted the pair duck through another door, which they closed behind them. George crept up and pressed his ear against the wood. From within came the sounds of fumbling, and murmurs too low for George to make out the words. Sevigny's voice—low, insistent. Cecile's, softer, higher. Was she arguing with him? Had Rossignol sold her to this villain against her will? Perhaps even as payment for his gambling debts?

Burning with righteous anger, George inched the door open a crack.

Inside stood a four-poster-bed covered with an ivory bedspread. Through the half-closed curtains, George could just make out Cecile lying on the bed, her dress in disarray. Sevigny crouched above her, leering like a filthy incubus. He pawed at her breast, yanking the white fabric aside to expose her bare nipple, then moved downwards, shoving her skirts up around her waist. She wore no petticoats, and Sevigny buried his face between her parted legs. George was ready to intervene, but the sighs that punctuated Cecile's breathing stopped him. If the Comte's attentions had been unwanted before, they weren't now. She was enjoying it.

Sevingy lifted his head. "Excitable little slut, aren't you?" He ran a finger over Cecile's pink slit. "Nice and wet for me already."

Cecile whimpered, arching her back, gripping the bedspread. George's blood rushed in his ears. Even as jealousy gripped his chest like an iron hand, the sight of her in such a state of disarray kindled his desire.

Sevigny unlaced his trousers, withdrawing his engorged member. The lascivious look on his face made George ill, but it could not dampen his arousal. Not while Cecile squirmed on the bed, one hand gripping her exposed breast, the other slipping between her legs as though she could wait no longer for her pleasure. But as Sevigny prepared to enter her, she stopped him.

"No," she said. "I want to be on top."

Sevigny frowned, but Cecile sat up, insisting, so he lay down on the bed, and allowed her to lower herself onto him. She let out a little groan as he filled her up, and George, transfixed, found his hand unconsciously drifting towards his manhood, just as he had at Rossignol's performance. After a few guilty strokes, he forced himself to stop. Someone could stumble upon him here at any moment. Cecile or Sevigny could look up and spot him. But the two of them seemed entirely engrossed in what they were doing, and the sight of her—oh, God! What he wouldn't give to be the one beneath her, buried deep inside her, feeling the motion of her body flow over him like a wave.

He glanced down the empty hallway. This surely wouldn't take long, not in the state he was in. He loosened his trousers and stifled a gasp as flesh met inflamed flesh. His eyes fixed on Cecile, he slid his hand up and down his hardness in time with the movements of her hips. The faster her thrusts, the louder her moans, the harder he stroked, bringing himself close to the edge before backing off and slowing down again. All his fears of discovery were soon forgotten.

Sevigny gripped Cecile's waist, thrusting his hips up to meet her as she ground into him. She was transformed, a creature of pure animal desire, her hair hanging wildly around her shoulders, her head thrown back in ecstasy. George was close to losing control when she happened to turn her head, and their eyes met. In one pointed glance she took in his state, and leaned deliberately forward, grasping Sevigny's shoulders and arching her back.

"Ahh, fuck me faster, you filthy whore," the Comte cried. "Don't slow down now."

But Cecile would not be rushed. Without taking her eyes off George's, she smiled, and reached down through a slit in her dress. As George quivered on the brink of ecstasy, she lifted something sharp and shining above her head, and plunged it down, straight into Sevigny's throat, again and again.

The Comte let out a strangled cry, blood pooling up from his fresh wound and onto the ivory sheets.

"Stop! No, stop!" Fumbling with his trousers, George rushed into the room and tried to wrestle the dagger from her hand. Blood soaked her white dress. Beneath her, the Comte twitched, fingers grasping, eyes rolling back in his head. A crimson bubble rose from his throat with his last breath, and he grew still.

Cecile turned to George, grinning, and let the dagger drop.

"You... you killed him." George backed away, his stomach turning.

Cecile ran a finger through the blood oozing from Sevigny's throat and licked it, leaving a spot of bright red on her lips.

"Come here and kiss me," she purred.

George remembered the metallic taste of blood in his mouth from the night they'd slept together, and a dream-like compulsion pushed him to take a few steps towards her. She slipped off the bed and met him in the middle of the room, kissing him hungrily, feverishly, her tongue exploring his mouth. Her hand dropped to his crotch.

"Still hard," she moaned. "You liked it."

She fell to her knees, and in an instant George was harder than ever. Glancing up at him, Cecile swirled her tongue around his head.

"Tell me you want it," she whispered.

George's gaze strayed to the still-warm body on the bed. "I... I can't."

Cecile ran her tongue down his full length, and back up again. "Tell me."

He did—that was the worst of it. She cupped his swollen balls with one hand, looking up at him enticingly through those blue eyes, and every barrier he'd tried to erect crumbled.

"I want it," he croaked.

Cecile stood, weaving her way back up his body to kiss him again. George took her by the waist, pushing her up against the nearest wall, and slid himself inside of her. She wrapped her legs around him, gasping.

"Hard! Do it hard! Oh, God."

The stench of blood filled his senses as he replayed, in his mind, the image of Cecile stabbing Sevigny. The way she'd plunged the knife down into his throat. The look of madness in her eyes. He licked her shoulder, where a splatter of red still lingered on her skin, and bit down on her soft flesh.

"Ahhh!" Cecile's body convulsed around him, and George came, hard, pinning her against the wall. He grabbed hold of her hand and kissed her again, and for a moment their hearts seemed to beat as one.

Cecile slipped from his grasp and planted her feet back onto the floor, wrapping her arms around his neck. He held her, shaking, his face buried in her hair.

"Well, well," came a voice from behind them. "This is a mess."

CHAPTER TWELVE

Cece untangled her arms from around George's neck. Her fingers found the choker, and she tugged it off. Weakness flooded her limbs. She slumped against the wall, her head reeling at the sight of the Comte's mangled body on the bed. Dark spots invaded her vision.

"Cecile!" George caught her just before she fainted. She looked up at him through the cloud of black, trying to make sense of what had just happened.

She'd killed Sevigny. She remembered it dimly, the way one might remember a drunken night after waking up the following morning. Heat rushed up her chest, prickling her face. Her heart raced. What had she done?

"Cecile," George repeated, more gently.

Cece looked into his eyes, and read his concern and confusion. But she also read the lingering sparks of dying lust. He'd watched her do this… this deed, and he'd enjoyed it. Maybe despite himself, but nevertheless. The way he'd fucked her… a shiver ran through her at the thought. The woman who'd done those things was not her. Surely he must know that?

"Don't you see me?" she asked.

George winced and turned away, letting her go. Unsteadily, she crossed the floor to Rossignol, who waited in the doorway.

"What are we going to do? Sevigny… I don't know what came over—"

"Put the necklace back on." Rossignol's command was irresistible, and the choker was halfway to her throat before she realized what she was doing.

"No." She pulled it away again. "I won't."

"Now, my dear, you'll feel better if you do."

"I won't!" Cece looked desperately at George, willing him to help her somehow, but he only stood with his head in his hands.

"The boy is useless to you," Rossignol said, his gaze locked on George. "Look up, Mr. Dashwood. Look at me."

George's jaw tightened. For a moment, Cece thought he would refuse, but then, slowly, he lifted his head, meeting Rossignol's eyes defiantly.

"You followed Cecile and Sevigny when they left the party," the puppet master said, softly. "You found them here together, interrupted them, and attacked the Comte in a fit of jealousy. You will stay here, in this room, and lock the door after we leave. When they come for you, you will confess your guilt. Do you understand?"

George didn't answer.

"Do you understand?"

"I—I…" George's eyes widened, still fixed on Rossignol's. He stood rigid and immobile, unable to force the words from his mouth.

"Unless you want to see Mademoiselle Dulac taken to the Bastille, you will confess," Rossignol repeated, his voice curling from the back of his throat like smoke. "Now… sleep."

George dropped his head, his shoulders slumping. Rossignol turned back to Cece.

"Put it on."

Cece lifted the necklace again, watching her hand move, powerless to stop it. The moment the ribbon touched her skin, the tension in her body dissipated. The warm, golden glow flooded through her limbs once more, and nothing else mattered.

"Come now, Selena," said Rossignol, and Cece's lips twisted into a smile. He held out his hand, and she took it, his warm fingers wrapping around hers. She walked with him to the door, each footstep echoing hollowly in the near-silent room. Her mind drifted, her thoughts floating away on a calm sea. Resistance seemed difficult. Exhausting. Perhaps it was easier to simply curl up in a corner of her mind and rest.

As she left the room, she cast one last glance at George. He watched her helplessly, wretchedness etched on his face. His image flickered and blurred, as if he were sinking into dark water, falling out of reach. Or perhaps it was her who was sinking. She was cold.

Too cold. An icy fear gripped her, and she tried to stop walking, but couldn't. Her limbs were numb, as though they no longer belonged to her. She was powerless. Her view blurred a dark red, and she realized she was looking out from within the ruby necklace.

CHAPTER THIRTEEN

George sat in Sevigny's chamber and waited to be discovered. A thick fog saturated his thoughts, and he could do nothing but stare at Sevigny's corpse, still cooling on the bed. How had he come to be here? He'd followed Cecile from the party. Watched her from behind the door. After that, he recalled nothing.

He closed his eyes, but an incessant banging made his head ache. It was only when the door splintered and he opened his eyes to see the Comte's friends spilling into the room that he realized what it was. They stood over him, an array of angry, shouting faces, and demanded an explanation.

Confess, whispered a voice in George's mind. The word stood out clearly from his confusion, as though edged in silver. *Confess*.

So he did. Like an automaton, he recited how he had watched his beloved being ravaged by Sevigny. How he had rushed in to protect her and grabbed a dagger he found on the floor. How he had stabbed the Comte in the throat. And as he told the story, it sharpened in his mind. He had done it. He remembered it all.

The Comte's friends shackled him and dragged him to Sevigny's wine cellar, threw him inside and locked the door.

George submitted to his imprisonment without a murmur, curling up in a corner of the pitch-dark cellar to await his fate. But the longer he sat on the cold flagstones, the less certain his thoughts became. The image of Cecile lifting the dagger flashed through his mind and, in its wake, his true memories flooded in. Cecile plunging the knife down. Her look of crazed delight. George recoiled from the thought. That wasn't her. Couldn't have been. The woman he'd watched murder the Comte—the woman he'd made love to—was surely Selena all along.

He no longer cared what happened to him. He had failed Cecile. Betrayed her. He remembered the fear and confusion in Cecile's eyes when she'd removed the necklace. She'd begged for his help, and he'd done nothing. He had simply stood by as Selena's spirit subsumed the woman he loved.

No doubt the Comte's family would call for him to be executed without trial. If that were the case, he wouldn't fight it. Anything he could say to prove his innocence would only incriminate Cecile. At least this way, he could go to his death knowing he was protecting her. If there was anything left of her to protect.

The night wore on, and George fell into a fitful doze. How long he slept, he had no idea, but eventually he woke to the sound of the door scraping on the flagstones. He sat up as the shaft of light from the hallway widened. A candle entered, closely followed by the hand holding it. George squinted.

"Bastian?"

"Shh!" Bastian closed the door behind him. "I'm breaking you out of here." He crouched to unlock George's shackles. "After they found the Comte's body, the place was in total confusion. I heard them talking about you and managed to slip these keys from the butler's room while the rest of them were running around in a panic. Had to wait 'til things calmed down before I could sneak back in. Come on, better be quick."

George staggered to his feet and headed for the door, but Bastian shook his head. "Not that way."

He led the way deeper into the cellar. Shadows loomed from all sides, thick and impenetrable.

"Are you sure we can get out this way?" George hissed.

"Must be somewhere around here," Bastian muttered, scouring the floor between shelves of dusty bottles. Eventually, the candlelight caught the edge of something metallic on the ground—the ring of a trapdoor.

"Help me." Bastian put down the candle and crouched to tug at the handle. George joined him, but for a moment, all their straining seemed to be in vain. Finally, one last pull wrenched it open, and the two of them fell back, panting.

George held the candle close to the black hole, revealing a ladder stretching down into the abyss.

"Where in God's name is this going to take us?"

"Stop complaining and get down there."

Navigating the ladder whilst holding the candle was difficult, but a few steps down, George found a candle-holder attached to the wall, and a moment later his feet touched solid ground. In the murk, he could just make out a large chamber with an arched ceiling. An underground river rushed alongside them. Bastian hopped down from the ladder and grabbed the candle.

"There should be a boat around here somewhere," he said, moving the light in a slow circle.

"Here!" George spotted a small rowing boat tethered at the bottom of a flight of steps. They clambered in and untied the ropes. Bastian pushed off from the shore, and as the boat bobbed along in the river's flow, George allowed himself to relax a little.

"What is this place?"

"These underground rivers are used to transport deliveries around the city," Bastian explained. "We should be able to find somewhere for you to hide while things settle down. I have some influence. Just give me a chance to speak to the right people."

"What happened to Cecile? Did you see her leave?"

Bastian shook his head, his face shadowy in the candlelight. "Nobody saw her or Rossignol. I suppose they slipped away before the fracas. What the hell happened, old fellow? People said you'd been found all but clutching the dagger that killed Sevigny."

"It was Cecile," George admitted. "I watched her do it. But it wasn't her fault! He's controlling her somehow. Rossignol, I mean. That performance—the spirit he conjured—I don't think it ever left. Whoever this Selena was, she's using Cecile's body now for her own ends, and I…"

He stopped, hanging his head.

"You what?"

"I betrayed her. I didn't realize. No, that's not right. I knew, but I didn't care. Not at that moment. I was weak, Bastian. So weak. I should have stopped her, and I didn't. Now I've lost Cecile, and who knows if she can be brought back again?"

"Spirits? Possession?" Bastian looked unconvinced. "We must concern ourselves first with keeping you out of prison, then perhaps we can worry about what has happened to Cecile. If she's even worth your concern. She left you to take the blame, after all."

"That's what I'm saying! It wasn't her," George replied. "Cecile wouldn't do that to me."

"She's a whore. An actress. It's her job to make you think she loves you. Some of them are very good at it, but the fact of the matter is, all they truly love is money. I feel for you, old fellow, but that's the way it is."

What was the use in arguing? George sat back in the boat, watching the candlelight flicker on the damp walls as Bastian steered them towards another set of steps. When they got close enough, Bastian leapt out and grabbed the craft's rope to moor it.

"I think we've gone far enough." He led the way up the steps to a metal door, which he pushed open with some difficulty, wedging his shoulder against it to gain purchase on the heavy iron.

Bones lined the corridor within from floor to ceiling, stretching off as far as the light allowed them to see. Shuddering, George followed his friend until they reached a tomb-like chamber walled by skulls.

"Not the most welcoming of spots," Bastian admitted, "but you're not likely to be disturbed here." He glanced at the candle, which was almost burnt out. "I'm sorry, I'll have to leave you without a light, or I'll have no way of finding my way back."

George shivered. "You're not going to leave me here?"

"I'll return in the morning with candles and supplies," Bastian replied. "Try to get some sleep."

George sat down and watched the light disappear down the corridor, along with the crunching of Bastian's footsteps, until both vanished into the distance. Then, feeling that he had only exchanged one prison for another, he lay down and stared into the darkness.

The cloak of black around him seemed solid enough to touch. He peered into it, trying to see the skulls lining the walls, each one a life extinguished. Each one a potential spirit, like the one who now haunted Cecile. And who was she, this Selena? Where had she come from? What had happened to her?

A memory of Cecile's words came back to him: the first time she'd been possessed, Rossignol had asked Selena how she'd died.

"I drowned myself... My husband drove me to it. I had no choice!"

Where had he heard something similar? His mind raced, and all at once it came to him.

Sevigny's wife. Somebody at the party had said she'd drowned herself, and suggested that Rossignol was somehow involved. They'd called her merely "the Comtesse", but what was her first name? Could it have been...?

"Bastian!" he yelled, getting to his feet and stumbling through the darkness as fast as he dared in the direction his friend had gone. "Bastian, wait!"

CHAPTER FOURTEEN

A girl in a blood-drenched dress walked into the darkened ballroom at Chateau Rossignol. Her hair was in disarray, her face and arms splattered with scarlet. A single candle flickered in her hands.

Cece watched her from afar.

The girl looked like her. She had Cece's face and Cece's body. But her eyes were colder, her movements sharper, more deliberate. She cast her gaze around the room with the air of an owner returning to a long-abandoned home.

Puzzled, Cece raised a hand in front of her face. Nothing happened. She looked down where her body ought to be. There was nothing to see. When she tried to move, a solid, invisible barrier blocked her path. And then she realized; she was on the other side of the mirrored wall. At least, whatever was left of her was. She had travelled back in the carriage, her view tinged with red, looking out from within the ruby that nestled around her throat. Now she could move more freely, up and down the room, but only within the mirrors—never beyond them.

Rossignol entered, footsteps echoing off the wooden floor. The girl in the blood-drenched dress turned to face him, smiling. Her smile was not like Cece's, either. Not the inviting, flirtatious smile she'd become famous for. Something far colder. More predatory.

"Selena." Rossignol slipped his hands around the girl's waist. "Is it truly you?"

"It will be," Selena replied, in Cece's voice. "Soon enough."

"And Cecile Dulac?"

"She grows weaker." Selena rose onto her tiptoes to kiss Rossignol on the lips. "I hardly sense her presence at all."

No! I'm here! I'm here!

Cece slammed her fists against the inside of the glass—but she had no fists. She screamed until her throat should have been raw—but no sound emerged.

I'm here! Let me out!

Rossignol clutched Selena's waist. "Then we have succeeded? I cannot—I must not—lose you again."

"You don't need to fear anything anymore," Selena purred. "Not if we complete the final ritual."

"The final...?" Rossignol frowned. "Rosie gave me to understand that the ruby was all that was needed."

Rosie! Had she been involved somehow, all along?

Selena put a finger to Rossignol's lips. "Shh, my love. I require just one more thing to complete my possession of this body and banish Cecile Dulac forever. All I need is an audience."

"Another party?"

"As many guests as you can persuade. Their life forces feed my energy. And tell them..." She fixed her gaze on his, a chilly glint in her eyes. "Tell them tomorrow's performance will be the most shocking yet."

A slow smile crept across Rossignol's face. He took her head in his hands and kissed her, pulling her close. Cece turned away, but behind her was only darkness.

It called to her, that darkness, with a siren song. Part of her longed to walk into it. Escape this hellish limbo. It was so cold here. So very cold.

But the flicker of the candlelight drew her attention back to the living world, and she stared at it until the light burned onto her eyeballs. If only she could absorb some of its warmth.

Rossignol swept Selena's hair aside to kiss her neck, and as he did, a faint tingle ran over Cece's skin.

I can feel!

She pressed herself up against the mirror as Rossignol slid the dress from Selena's shoulders.

"I missed you so," he murmured. "I wished I had died with you."

Selena embraced him, her arms around his neck. "No more sorrow, my love. My husband is gone and I am here. We can be free."

As he ran the backs of his fingers down her arms, Cece felt his touch. She felt the material as it slid over her breasts, leaving her nipples exposed. The sensation was slight, as though her limbs were numb and deadened, but it was there. Touch by touch, kiss by kiss, she crept back into her body. Every tiny caress left her desperate for more. Pain, pleasure—it was all the same to her. Something—anything—was better than the numbness.

Selena turned her back to Rossignol, letting her dress fell to the floor. His hardness pressed against her buttocks. His hands roved over her stomach. Cupped her breasts. He pinched her nipples and Selena—or was it Cece?—let out a gasp.

They battled for possession of her body. With every encroachment Cece made, Selena resisted, her mind a dark force pushing Cece back into numbness. But the more Rossignol touched her, the more real Cece felt. She leaned into him as he slipped a hand between her legs, wanting his touch. Wanting more. As he toyed with her, explosions went off all over her body.

"Oh, Alexandre," she heard herself murmur. But it wasn't Cece speaking. It was still Selena. To find her way back, fully, she would need something more.

From the corner of her eye, Cece saw herself in the mirror, her reflection pale and ghostly. When he withdrew his hand, she slipped back into that dark water, the icy tendrils closing around her limbs.

But Rossignol only paused for long enough to unlace his trousers, and when he slid his cock between Cece's legs, her consciousness crept back into her body. With each thrust the sensation intensified a little more, and when Rossignol gripped her hair, it was Cece, not Selena, who moaned at the tug on her scalp. When he spanked her, hard, it was Cece who yelped with delight. She focused on the pleasure building inside her, coiling tighter and tighter like a spring, and began to force Selena out of her mind, piece by tiny piece.

As her orgasm built, she reached for the necklace, fumbling through the waves of ecstasy washing over her. Her fingers found the velvet ribbon. But where was the catch? She groped deliriously, but it was no use. The choker tightened around her throat. She couldn't breathe. Her body stiffened, thrumming like a tight string.

Her toes curled. She was about to come, and she couldn't, couldn't, couldn't get it off.

Another thrust. Another spank, and the sensation of being hit while Rossignol's cock filled her sent Cece over the edge. As her body convulsed and her legs grew weak, she heard him grunt, and felt him come inside her, and then…

Nothing.

Nothing.

She was gone. Distant, watching from behind the mirror. She howled with frustration and disappointment as every sensation tore from her at once, leaving her cold and empty, floating in the freezing void.

On the other side of the mirror, in the ballroom's glow, Selena sighed with satisfaction, turning to kiss Rossignol as he withdrew. Cece hammered her ghostly fists on the glass, and screamed, and screamed, and screamed.

CHAPTER FIFTEEN

"Yes, the Comte's wife was named Selena," Bastian said, as George ushered him back through the catacombs to the underground river. "Are you saying you think she is this spirit?"

"Some of your friends seemed to think Rossignol was involved in her death."

"There was a rumor that they had an affair." Bastian located the boat, and the two of them clambered in.

"Tell me everything you know about her."

"She was the Comte's second wife," Bastian said, as he unhooked the rope and pushed off into the river. "There was rather a scandal when he married her. She was a dancer at the Palais Theatre—like your Cecile—and the Comte took a fancy to her. First, he installed her as his courtesan. Later, when his first wife died, he married her. Nobody could account for it. Why would he marry his whore? Witchcraft was suggested."

George's eyes widened. "Witchcraft?"

If he hadn't been busy trying to row the boat, Bastian would no doubt have shrugged, in his Gallic way.

"Some people think that when a whore seduces a rich man, witchcraft must be involved. Me, I suspect it was far simpler. The Comte was weak-minded, and the Comtesse, by all accounts, was a very persuasive woman."

"Did you ever meet her?"

"No. I was too young to be going to society parties. But I heard all about it when she killed herself."

"Drowned herself. That's what the spirit said."

"Drowned herself, yes." Bastian narrowed his eyes at George. "You understand, old fellow, that when we step out from these catacombs, you're risking arrest for murder. And I, for breaking you out. And still you talk about spirits."

"When Rossignol resurrected Selena," George said, "she told us someone had driven her to it; that she wanted revenge. Now Sevigny's dead. If she and Rossignol really were having an affair, well, I believe now he's found a way to bring her back. His dead love. And now she's killed her husband. She's had the revenge she wished for. What if Rossignol means to keep her here, at Cecile's expense?"

"Even supposing all this is the case, how do we get her back?"

"I don't know. But I suspect the necklace is the source of Selena's power. It's only when she removes it that Cecile regains control of herself. I'm going to head for Chateau Rossignol, and figure out a way to get it off Cecile. You leave ahead of me. I'll wait a good while before I venture out. Nobody need know you had anything to do with this."

Bastian steered the boat towards the bank. "That night in the cellar's addled your brain, old fellow. Resurrected spirits? Rossignol's a showman, that's all. An old fraud." He tied the boat up again and hopped out.

"How long has he been doing these sordid little shows of his?" George asked, following his friend up a flight of steps.

"As long as I can recall."

"Since before Selena's death?"

"I believe so. People say it's how he made his money."

They emerged into a narrow alleyway, blinking in the early morning light. The streets were already busy with market sellers and office clerks on their way to work, and the two of them easily melted into the crowd.

"Perhaps Selena was involved in the shows somehow," George mused. "Perhaps they discovered something together. Some occult key." He frowned. "It must have to do with the necklace. I don't think we should go straight there. I think we need to talk to somebody who knows more about what happened between Rossignol, Selena and Sevigny."

"Rosie," said Bastian.

"What?"

"She's known Rossignol for years. She was his protege when she was only a child. She must have some idea of what really happened."

"Then we have to go back to the theatre and find her."

Bastian gripped George's arm. "No. We can't have you walking around in broad daylight."

"How can I sit still when Cecile's very existence may be in danger?"

"You can, because you must. You won't be much use to your paramour if you've had your head taken off by Monsieur Guillotine. Come with me. I know somewhere you can lie low. I'll bring Rosie to you there."

Bastian led the way through the marketplace, weaving through the crowd until he reached a small, unobtrusive door tucked between an apothecary and a bakery. Inside was a shabby parlor where a damp, musty smell hung in the air. Several young ladies lounged there, dressed in little more than underclothes. They looked George and Bastian up and down as they entered.

"It's a bit early, isn't it?" piped up an older woman sitting at a rickety desk.

"We're not here for your services," Bastian replied. "My friend here needs a place to stay for the day. He's awaiting a visitor."

The woman narrowed her eyes at him. "I don't want any trouble."

"Look at him." Bastian smirked. "Does he look as though he'll cause you trouble?"

She frowned at George, then shrugged.

"Nevertheless…" She held out her hand.

Bastian rolled his eyes, but withdrew his purse and handed her a few sous. She smiled, showing blackened teeth, and gestured for George to take a seat on the nearby couch.

"Get some sleep," Bastian told him, before hurrying out again. George lay on the couch, certain he was too anxious to sleep, but exhaustion had taken its toll, and within a few minutes he fell into a fitful slumber.

CHAPTER SIXTEEN

When George woke, daylight was already fading. Men of all ages and stations filled the parlor: lounging, drinking, sharing bawdy jokes with the girls. He was surprised they'd allowed him to take up one of their sofas for so long.

"Ah, there you are, sleepyhead." The madam sashayed over. Her ringlets had fallen flat over the course of the day, and her rouged cheeks looked more false than ever against her pale skin. "Your friends are waiting for you."

She led George into a small side room, set up for gambling. There, on an old armchair, Rosie perched on Bastian's lap, purring sweet nothings into his ear. Both looked up as George entered.

"Have you no sense of urgency?" George snapped. "Why didn't you wake me?"

"I tried. You were dead to the world." Bastian seemed more interested in caressing Rosie's neck. "Besides, I thought you ought to have your sleep. When you hear what Rosie has to say, you'll understand why you must have your wits about you."

George took a seat opposite them. "And what does Rosie have to say?"

"Monsieur Rossignol would be dreadfully upset if he knew I had betrayed his confidence," Rosie said, pouting a little, as Bastian kissed his way along her collarbone.

"How much do you want?"

"Twenty francs."

"Consider it done." George leaned forward. "Now tell me: what do you know about Selena?"

Rosie slipped off Bastian's lap and onto the arm of the chair, turning her attention fully, if reluctantly, to George.

"When Monsieur Rossignol first came to Paris, he procured me to help him with his act. I was only fourteen then. My job was to pretend to be hypnotized."

"Pretend? So there was no truth to it?" The thought sent a shock-wave through George's heart. Had Cecile been pretending all this time? Had he never truly known her at all?

"Not then. It was a performance, nothing more. Monsieur would speak a few words and perform a bit of meaningless drama, and I would make a show of being under his control. I learned to act like a doll, doing exactly as I was told. I learned to make my eyes blank and my face expressionless. I even learned how to take these burns," she held out her scarred arm, "without flinching in the slightest. You saw it all, the night you watched us."

"You were very convincing," George said, his mouth dry.

Rosie shrugged. "I have had a great deal of practice."

"And these performances were all… like the one we saw?"

"Oh, at first it was much more innocent. I would lift my skirt and show my ankles, or be persuaded to kiss a man in the audience on the cheek. But the audiences were wild for it. They wanted more, more, more! More flesh. More titillation. It was nothing they couldn't have seen in the privacy of this very whorehouse, for half the fee, but it was the illusion of hypnotism they craved. They really believed I was entirely under Monsieur's power; that I would have done anything he asked. Or at least they wanted to believe. Who cares which? The idea of having a pretty young woman dancing to one's tune like a puppet on a string is a fantasy for many men, I suppose."

George's gut twisted, clenched by a cold fist. Had he really been taken in by an elaborate ruse?

"Tell Dashwood what you told me," Bastian cut in. "About the Comte."

"Oh yes, of course." Rosie's face brightened. "One evening, the Comte du Sevigny was in the audience, along with his comely young wife. Oh my, what a picture she was. You never saw anything like her. Green eyes that glittered like emeralds. Raven-dark hair. A body that begged to be naked, and those lips… Monsieur Rossignol wanted her right away, and how could I blame him? I have always been an admirer of the female form, you know, Monsieur

Dashwood. I'm not ashamed to admit it, though it may be unnatural in one of my sex. But the Comtesse du Sevigny was beautiful, and my master became obsessed. He would have her. He must have her. She was his only desire."

"What did Rossignol do?" George asked.

"He requested me to arrange an assignation with her one evening. She wasn't difficult to persuade. Selena was terribly bored with that old drunkard, and fascinated by Monsieur Rossignol's act. She saw through it, of course, but she taught him her secrets. She taught him how to call upon the spirit world."

"Then there was a way?"

"Oh, yes."

"How?"

Rosie laughed. "Of course she never told me! Why would she? All Selena ever cared about was being famous. She became part of the act, you know. Only on nights when her husband was with his gambling friends, and she knew he would not attend. The performance was a thrill for her. She even had all those mirrors installed in the ballroom, so she could see herself. Oh, the two of us together…" Rosie sighed, a dreamy expression crossing her face. "We drew the crowds in a way I could never have done alone."

"But the Comte found out?"

Rosie grimaced. "How could he not? All of Paris was ablaze with talk about the Comtesse. Her beauty. Her wildness. She held séances on stage in the ballroom. Attracted spirits to possess her and let men from the audience fuck her in front of everybody. Of course her husband heard, and one night he came to see for himself whether it was true. He found his wife tied to a cross, with a man on either side of her." Rosie stifled a laugh. "I suppose he was a little upset. They rowed. He dragged her out to his carriage and took her home to beat her. She escaped the next night and ran straight to Chateau Rossignol to show her bruises to Monsieur Rossignol. Unfortunately, Monsieur owed money to Sevigny. The Comte threatened to ruin him completely if he took Selena in."

Rosie faltered. A look of genuine grief passed across her pretty face. "My poor Selena. She was abandoned. She had nobody. She took herself out to the lake in the Chateau gardens, filled her pockets with stones, and walked out into the water. When he found out, Monsieur was distraught. But it was too late. He's been looking for a way to bring her back ever since."

"And now he's done it," said George. "But how? And how do we send her back to where she came from? The necklace—?"

"The necklace belonged to Selena, yes," Rosie said, anticipating his question. "Monsieur told me when conjuring a spirit, it helps to have one of their possessions near. It never worked on any other girl, though. At least, not for long. Cecile is different, I think. Monsieur wanted her particularly, I'm not sure why. But I do not think simply removing the necklace will banish Selena completely. Not now their souls have become so entwined."

"So what do we do?"

Rosie shrugged. "I am not sure."

"Cecile is your friend. Are you just going to leave her to be destroyed by this… this demon?"

Rosie jutted her chin. "Selena was no demon. Just a woman who wanted more than what she had. You men always think that women who want more are evil. All she wants is to live the life that was stolen from her."

"And I'm sorry for her. But she can't do that. Not at the expense of an innocent. Is there nothing you can think of that may help us?"

Rosie considered. "There may be something," she said at last. "I understand from the rituals I've participated in that for a spirit to fully inhabit a body, the body must be brought to a pinnacle of sensation."

"You mean…?"

"Orgasm." Seeing George's discomfort, Rosie laughed. "That moment of weakness and openness is when it is easiest for the spirit to fully possess someone. It is possible it may work the other way: that now Selena is in full possession of Cecile's body, Cecile's best chance to return to her body is during that peak. But it will not be easy for her. The moment it is over, her chance is lost. Selena will grow stronger and Cecile weaker still."

"How does it work? How can we be sure Cecile will take back control of her body in that… um… moment?"

"As to that," Rosie got to her feet, smoothing out her dress. "You men will scoff and call me sentimental."

"I can assure you, I am in no mood to scoff at any suggestion that might help."

"Very well. Selena once told me that the pull of love is stronger than death. You love Cecile, I think?"

"I do. Of course I do. But what does that mean? How can I help?"

"We should discuss it while we walk. You are in a hurry, no?"

"I am." George wrapped his scarf high around his neck to hide his face, and the three of them headed out, on their way to Chateau Rossignol.

CHAPTER SEVENTEEN

Cece watched from within the necklace as Selena dined with Rossignol that evening. Selena ate and drank little, instead talking breathlessly about how that evening's performance would be more exciting, more extreme than anything they had ever done before. Her anticipation thrummed through Cece's consciousness, like faint ripples passing over the surface of a lake. Try as she might to catch one of those waves of feeling, though, Cece found it impossible to use one as a way back into her body. They were too weak, dissolving the moment she directed her thoughts to them.

As Selena headed upstairs to dress, Cece followed her, flitting helplessly from mirror to mirror, settling once more in the necklace when there were no looking-glasses or shiny candlesticks at her disposal. Everywhere she went, the draw of the cold water was behind her, pulling her down. The view of her old body became hazier; the call of the depths more insistent.

When Selena reached the bedroom, she unlaced her gown and let it slip to the floor. She lit some candles and placed them in the shape of a pentagram on the floor, then stood in front of the mirror, assessing Cece's figure with a critical eye. From the other side of the mirror, Cece stared out at herself, the expression on her familiar features cold and aloof.

Selena bowed her head and muttered a few quiet words, then rubbed her hands together and ran them over her hair. Beneath her touch, it changed from waves of blonde to sleek black. Selena blinked, and Cece's blue eyes transformed to jade green. When she looked up again, her eyes met Cece's, and, to Cece's surprise, she shuddered.

"Go away," Selena said, in a low tone.

"Why are you doing this to me?" Cece's voice was little more than a whisper, but Selena seemed to hear her well enough. She leaned in close to the mirror.

"Because," she said, "I don't want to go back there."

"But why me?"

Selena smiled, baring white teeth. "I know you, little Cecile Dulac. I remember you. You wanted to be like me. Well, now you are. Now you'll see what it really means to follow in my footsteps."

"What does that mean?" Cece began, but Selena raised a finger to her lips.

"Shh. Quiet. I don't want you messing this up for me. Now go away!"

Selena flung the dress over the mirror, shrouding Cece in darkness again. Without her body to focus on, she lost all sense of up and down. There was nothing but the void, and the cold, and the darkness in every direction. Panic seized her, and she struggled against the rising tide, kicking and screaming as water filled her lungs.

Then she was inside the necklace again, and Selena was walking downstairs.

Cece breathed a sigh of relief—or would have, if she had lungs with which to breathe. She had to stay in the necklace. All this time she'd been praying Selena would take the choker off, to give her the chance to take possession of her body again. Now the necklace was the only thing keeping her from sinking straight into the cold depths from which Selena had come. They had changed places entirely. If Selena realized that, and understood that she no longer needed it, what would happen to Cece?

She glimpsed Selena as they passed a looking-glass on the stairs. She wore her newly black hair down around her shoulders and a scarlet, kimono-style dressing gown, loosely tied so every step showed off a sliver of leg. If Cece hadn't known the body was her own, she would never have recognized herself. It seemed the transformation was almost complete.

From the hall below, Rossignol was watching.

"How did you do this?" he asked, his voice thick with emotion. When Selena reached him, he ran his hands over her hair and face like a blind man trying to trace her features.

"A simple spell or two."

Rossignol shook his head in disbelief. "You are magnificent. But then, you always were."

Selena smiled her haughty, cruel smile and turned to the ballroom door. "Shall we?"

Her excitement shimmered as Rossignol pushed open the doors. Tiny pinpricks tingled at the tips of Cece's fingers and toes. Through her ruby-tinged lens, she saw the warped faces of the guests turn in their direction. Blood-red eyes, watching, wondering. Cece slipped into the mirrored walls where she could get a better look.

The scarlet of Selena's gown and the sable of her hair singled her out amidst the pastel colors worn by the other women. The simplicity of her kimono shone among the others' frills and flounces, and an expanse of china-white skin ran from her neck down her deep décolletage, smoother and more flawless than Cece's skin had ever been. The kimono hung on Selena's form perilously, as though it might slip off at any moment. No doubt that was exactly the point.

The crowd parted as Selena passed by. Rossignol rushed forward to help her ascend the steps, and she stood in the center of the stage, looking like the proud figurehead above the chateau's door. Cece sensed a crackle of electricity, like a lightning storm brewing beneath heavy clouds. Slowly but surely, the trail of sensation that would lead her back to her body illuminated. The air was so thick with anticipation she could almost taste it.

Selena's eyes roved over the crowd. Behind her, Rossignol directed a group of servants in hoisting a cross-shaped contraption onto the stage.

"My dear ladies and gentlemen," she began, in a clear, sing-song voice. "I hope you are all looking forward to tonight's show. Please, take your seats. I will require a volunteer." She walked the stage until her gaze landed on someone in the front row. "You, Mademoiselle?"

Cece recognized Rosie as she stepped up to the stage. So too, it seemed, did some patrons, who heartily cheered her appearance. Selena kissed her on both cheeks, her hand lingering on Rosie's waist.

Rosie didn't seem the least bit perturbed by Selena's changed appearance—almost as though she had expected it. Cece pressed up against the surface of the mirror, hoping to attract her friend's attention. But Rosie's eyes were on the crowd. Cece followed her gaze.

Wait, was that...?

She flitted down the rows of people to get a better look, straining to see from behind the mirror. It was! It was George, wearing a battered old top hat, his face half-hidden by a white scarf.

"George! George!" Cece banged on the mirror, but of course he could not hear her. Defeated, she slunk back to the top of the room, attracted by a tingle in her lips, to find Selena and Rosie locked in an embrace. She could just feel the brush of Rosie's lips on hers. Could just taste the sweetness of the wine her friend had been drinking. A tease. No more. Behind her, the cold fingers of the dark water made her shiver. The ballroom faded. As Selena grew stronger, her power strengthened by the attention of the crowd, Cece was losing her chance. She needed to find a way back to her body before it was too late.

"Ladies, ladies." Rossignol put one hand on Selena's shoulder, one on Rosie's, and the two women reluctantly broke from their kiss. "As delightful as it is to watch the two of you, we promised tonight's audience a little more than the ordinary."

"Of course." Selena's smile was demure, but as she looked at her erstwhile lover, a shot of anger flared through Cece. No, not just anger. Hatred. Fury. The same violent, murderous urge that had overcome her at the sight of Sevigny; quickly suppressed, but powerful nonetheless. It whipped through her consciousness, snapping her back into her body for one breathless instant.

Selena turned to the crowd. "Tonight, ladies and gentlemen, I have a story to tell you. An old folk tale, passed down to me by my mother, who heard it from her mother before her. A story of obsession and betrayal, and the cruelty of men."

Rossignol watched her nervously, gripping the head of his silver-topped cane. But he didn't dare interrupt, and Selena went on as the lights dimmed.

"In the forest, a long time ago, lived spirits who would dance a man to death. Beneath the light of a full moon, the ghosts of spurned women rose from their beds of earth and moss to charm unwary travelers into their embrace. They spared no man, no matter how innocent a life he had led.

"To the wraiths, all men were the same: treacherous, untrustworthy. Unworthy of life. Any fool who stumbled into their clutches found himself forced to dance with them the whole night long, until at last he expired from sheer exhaustion. Only if he could make it to sunrise—when the spirits were forced to disperse— would he survive."

Cece shivered. It was her aunt's story. The words were as familiar to her as if they had been written into her bones. She could almost hear herself as a child, asking, "Did any of them ever survive?"

And how? How did Selena know her aunt's tale? Word for word, just as Marthe had told it? Before she spoke again, Selena glanced at the mirror. Their eyes met; something passed across the bridge that bound them together, soul to soul, and all of a sudden, Cece understood.

"Tonight, gentlemen, we dance." Selena's mouth curled into a slow smile. "How many of you will survive until sunrise?"

CHAPTER EIGHTEEN

The men in the audience thought it a game, of course. George saw it in their eager expressions as they watched Selena. An attractive woman, playing the femme fatale for their entertainment. They hadn't seen what Selena had done to Sevigny. They didn't know that when the servants drew the curtains and locked the doors, it was for more than simply 'show'. Selena was serious when she said none of them should see the break of day.

"We have to get out of here," muttered Bastian.

"We can't. Not without Cecile." He'd come this far. There was no backing out now.

Rossignol stood to the side of the stage, watching Selena with a mixture of longing and fear. She beckoned him to her, and he untied her kimono, slipping it from her shoulders. If George hadn't known to whom the body truly belonged, he would not have recognized this lithe figure, with her raven-black hair and porcelain skin, as having anything to do with the Cecile he'd known.

Selena climbed onto the X-shaped rack and lay down, her arms and legs spread wide. "Tie me up."

Moving like an automaton, Rossignol wrapped ribbons around her wrists and ankles. Selena smiled indulgently. The performance seemed a familiar routine to both of them, but Rossignol's hands shook as he secured the bonds. The sight made George even more anxious. Just what kind of creature had Rossignol unleashed onto the world, if the puppet master himself was afraid of her?

"We need to find some way to get her alone," George whispered.

Bastian raised his eyebrows. "With so many people around?"

"I can hardly do... what I have to do here in front of everybody."

"You may have no choice." Bastian smirked. "I assure you, I would happily step in, but it is not I who is in love with poor Cecile, so it is not I who can recall her."

"Yes, yes I know." George rubbed his forehead. "Rosie was perfectly clear on that point. It takes a true lover to summon the spirit back into this realm, as Rossignol was for Selena."

"The question is, are you that prince?"

"The question is," George replied, "is this not just some fevered fairy tale imagining? Can Rosie possibly be correct?"

"There's only one way to find out."

George looked back at the stage. Rosie tied a blindfold around Selena's eyes, and Rossignol held a sharp knife, the blade glinting in the dim light.

"With my subject under hypnosis," he said, in a low voice that had the audience straining to hear, "I am master of her sensations. I control her pain. I control her pleasure. I can even," he placed the point of the knife to Selena's chest, just above her breast, "intermingle them."

The knife punctured Selena's skin, and she let out a gasp, straining against her bonds as a scarlet bead of blood formed on her pristine skin. George winced, wondering what torture Rossignol had in mind for her that night, and whether Cecile was aware of any of it.

Rosie stepped up to lick away the blood. She flicked her tongue over Selena's nipple, then kissed her—a kiss which Selena received hungrily, as though the taste of blood was as blissful to her as the pain. George turned away, and caught sight of a frightened face in the mirror nearest him—a face that was burned onto his heart. Her faint reflection rippled.

"Cecile!" he hissed, nudging Bastian. "She's there!"

But by the time his friend turned around, Cecile was gone. Rossignol lifted his knife once more, and, seized by sudden panic, George rushed down the aisle between the seats.

"Stop!" he cried. "Stop, this cannot go on. This must not go on." He pointed a shaking finger at Rossignol. "This man is evil, can't you see that?"

Rossignol lowered his knife. "Monsieur Dashwood," he said, smoothly. "To what do I owe this interruption?"

"I demand that you release Cecile." The words did not come out as strongly, nor as firmly, as he meant them to. At the edge of his vision, he was all too aware of Selena lying on the cross, naked and spreadeagled, her chest rising and falling as she breathed. He could feel her listening.

Rossignol didn't take his eyes off George. "This man is a murderer," he said, gesturing to his servants. "He killed the Comte du Sevigny. Restrain him."

But as the stagehands stepped up to take hold of George's arms, Selena's voice rang out.

"Wait."

Nobody moved. George knew he ought to seize his chance to do… something, but he was powerless to speak. He felt strange, distant, as though he couldn't quite recall why any of this mattered anymore.

"Rosie, untie me." Selena's voice was a point of light in a darkening room.

Rosie removed Selena's blindfold and unlaced the ribbons, helping her sit up. Selena stepped down from the contraption, head held high, loose hair partially concealing her breasts. The incongruous thought flashed across George's mind that she would make a perfect model for Eve in a painting, but it soon vanished. The moment he met her eyes, a fog descended upon him, blocking out that and all other thoughts.

"So pleased you could join us, Monsieur Dashwood." She glanced at the cross. "I suppose we will need somebody to take my place. The show must go on, after all."

Powerless to resist her enchantment, George made his way up to the cross. Cecile's pale face watched from the mirror. Some small inner voice told him he shouldn't be doing this, but he didn't care. Selena was beautiful—perfection itself. She was the one he'd loved all along, he was sure of it. He submitted serenely as Rosie removed his jacket, and lay back against the cross for her to fasten the ribbons around his wrists and ankles. Selena bent over him, her hair tickling his face, and kissed him on the cheek.

"There now. Isn't that better?" She ran a hand down his chest, raking her fingers over his crotch. "Now you can relax."

Yes. I can relax. His mind floated on a warm sea. The stunned expressions of the crowd bore no meaning at all. All his worries about Cecile; about Rossignol; about being arrested… all of it melted away. All that mattered was Selena. He would have done anything for her.

Slowly, she unlaced his trousers. George's manhood throbbed harder than it ever had before. Selena worked her hand over its length, teasingly at first, then faster, faster, until he was sure he could not hold back for a second longer. His orgasm built; his body clenched.

And she let go.

George groaned with disappointment, thrusting his hips to meet thin air. Selena laughed, then crouched to bring her head level with his manhood, blowing softly over its head. When she flicked her tongue over him, tasting his effluence, his body tensed, an explosion brewing.

But there would be no satisfaction for him this time. Selena stood and turned away. As George writhed on his cross, she approached Rossignol.

"Forgive me, Alexandre," she said, slipping the knife from between his fingers, "but I fear your show has become... how do they say it in England? *Old hat.* I think our audience would prefer something new."

With a flick of her hand, the mirrors around the walls darkened. A red mist descended over them, like blood flowing from the ceiling, bathing the room in an eerie scarlet glow. The crowd surged for the door, only to find that they were, indeed, locked in. Their frightened faces repeated in the mirrors, reflections of reflections, stretching away into infinity.

Selena laughed.

"I can't let you leave, I'm afraid. You see, while I was dead I made a few friends, and they would all like very much to return to the land of the living. Now is your chance, spirits! Come to me! Take these bodies for your own!"

The air crackled with energy. One by one the audience crumpled, dropping to their knees, howling the way Rosie and Cecile had when the spirits had first taken them. But unlike Rosie and Cecile, they never stood up again. Gradually, their bodies stilled, and the room fell silent. Selena stood with her arms outstretched, her face radiant, her expression ecstatic.

"Selena…" Rossignol gaped in horror. "This wasn't what we planned."

"I have their energy now. It feeds me. Makes me stronger. It's what you wanted, isn't it? To have me back?" With a satisfied sigh, Selena wrapped her arms around his neck. "How I missed you, Alexandre. Nobody ever understood me like you did." She kissed him, long and lingeringly, sliding his jacket from his shoulders as she did so. He remained motionless as she unbuttoned his shirt and kissed her way down his chest. As she crouched before him, looking up at him, she ran a finger over the bulge in his trousers.

"You loved me, didn't you?" she asked, her eyes wide and appealing.

"I did… I do." Rossignol's voice was choked. "Selena… consider all I've done to bring you back to me. Isn't that proof enough? I never loved anyone but you."

"Such sweet words." Selena untied his trousers and withdrew his manhood with a wicked smile. "You men are all full of such sweet words. But when I was alone? When I had nobody, nothing? Where were you, Alexandre? Worrying about your money!" She brandished the knife. "I hope this is sharp, for your sake."

"Selena! No!" Blanching, Rossignol tried to back away, but she held him tight, bringing the knife up to the base of his rapidly dying erection. As he twisted in her grip, wincing, Rosie wrapped her arms around his waist to hold him firm. Her eyes met Selena's in a moment of understanding.

George struggled, but even if he hadn't been bound, the effort would have been wasted. Like the eye of a storm, Selena held them all in thrall. All he could do was stare in horror as she sliced through Rossignol's penis.

Rossignol's howl cut through the silent room. He fell back against Rosie, weeping, gasping for air, clawing at her face and chest as he sank to his knees. He curled himself into a trembling ball, and Selena held up her prize. Blood flowed over her hand, down her arm.

"You see." She faced George. "You see what happens to men who betray their lovers?"

CHAPTER NINETEEN

Selena's fury blazed through Cece's veins. Stronger than pleasure, stronger than pain, it lit up the path back to her body like lanterns along a roadside. Connected once more with her flesh, she held the knife as it sliced through Rossignol's organ, and found a kind of affinity—a sisterhood—with the mind directing it.

Now you understand. We will be stronger together.

When she'd heard Selena recite her aunt's story, the truth had become clear to Cece. She'd come to Paris following in her Aunt Marthe's footsteps, only to find that nobody recognized the name. It was as though the aunt who had written letters back home about her glorious rise to fame had never existed.

And she hadn't. At least, not in Paris. Because Marthe changed her name. Understanding dawned on Cece as her thoughts merged with Selena's. Marthe was the woman who left Cece's village, but Selena had arrived in Paris. Selena was the one who had joined the ballet, become a star, and eventually married a rich man. Selena, who had needed Cece specifically—a kindred body, easier to possess.

As Selena held her bloody prize above her head, Cece's mind filled with all the injustices meted out to her by mankind, and Selena's rage became her own. When she turned to George with her warning, she looked through her own eyes, spoke with her own voice, and when Selena raised Rossignol's discarded cane high above his head, it was Cece who brought it down. She understood now. The betrayal, the suffering her aunt had endured. They were not enemies. It was men who had tried to make them so.

She brought the cane down on its owner's head, again and again, until his cries died away and his body twitched and stilled. Tossing it to one side, she laughed at George, squirming in his bonds.

"Poor boy." She ran a bloody finger over his lips.

He watched her, wide-eyed, trembling. "Cecile?"

"Oh, you see me now, do you?" Cece laughed. "Yes, of course you do. See me, George Dashwood. See me for what I am."

"This isn't you."

"No, you're wrong. This is me. It's just not the me you wanted to believe in." She stood on tiptoe, licked the blood from his lips, then slipped her tongue into his unwilling mouth, waiting for the moment that he gave in. For the moment that his desire overcame his fear, and his resistance dissolved. The moment she felt it, she pulled back.

"This is Selena's influence," he managed.

"You're right. It is. I can't tell anymore where I end and she begins. And I feel..." she leaned in to whisper in his ear, "so much better."

She danced her fingers over George's flaccid cock, and turned to Rosie. Their eyes met, Rosie interpreting her wish with the intuition of a long-term collaborator.

"Sit." Rosie approached Bastian where he stood, still mesmerized. He sank into the nearest seat and she straddled him, lowering her lips to his. Her hand found his crotch and she freed his manhood, caressing him with slow strokes. She lifted her hips and took him inside her; his hands pawing at her breasts, roving over her back.

As Cece hoped, George's body responded to the sight, his cock stiffening once more. She crawled on top of him.

"You want me," she whispered, poising herself above him, just grazing his tip. "You can have me, one last time."

"No."

"No?" She slid herself down onto him, moaning as he filled her. "I don't think I want to hear you speak anymore." A fire burned at the base of her spine, building with every thrust.

"I know you, Cecile. I see you. This isn't you."

Boiling with frustration, Cece raised her knife to his throat. "I was going to make this as pleasant for you as I could, but you're trying my patience. You'll die tonight, George Dashwood. You'll die like all the rest of them."

"Perhaps I will." As Cece ground into him, George brought his hips up to meet her as best he could, speaking between ragged breaths. "But I'll die loving you. Maybe that will be enough."

"Enough for what?"

"Enough to free you."

She looked into his eyes, and the simple sincerity there caused a flutter deep in her chest. She dismissed it: those were old feelings, Cece's feelings. *You were a fool to love him*, Selena whispered in her mind. *They are all the same.* The memory of his betrayal was still sharp, and she leaned forward, fucking him harder in her anger.

His betrayal, or Rossignol's? Cece was no longer sure where Selena's memories ended, and hers began. Her head swam. Desperately, she cast about for something to cling to in the midst of the storm of emotions engulfing her. Selena's bitterness, Selena's fury, Selena's vengeance. It was too much for this body to hold.

"The sun is rising," George said.

Cece glanced at the window. Shafts of light broke through the heavy curtains. Panic gripped her. Selena's panic. She had left it too late. There was no more time. She had to kill him now, before the dawn broke.

And still she hesitated.

"No," she gasped, pressing the knife against his flesh, unsure if she was trying to convince him, or herself. "No, you're just like the rest of them."

"Then kill me. But you'd better do it quickly."

Cece grimaced. *Condemn him*, her aunt screamed. *They are all the same. They are all liars.* But, looking at him, she saw the sweet boy she'd first met. The one who'd convinced her he was different. Had that all been an illusion?

He's a liar. A betrayer, like the rest of them. Kill him!

But if she killed him, she would never be sure. Perhaps it didn't matter. Perhaps what mattered more was that she, Cecile Dulac, was no murderer.

The thought rang through her mind, a pinpoint of clarity amidst the tempest of rage. *I am Cecile Dulac, and I am no murderer.* She slowed her movements, violent lust transforming into a breathless, fragile ecstasy.

"You came back for me," she said, looking into George's eyes.

"Of course I did."

"I left you to take the blame for Sevigny, and you came back anyway."

"You needed me," George said. "I was wrong to treat you as I did, but I wouldn't leave you if—if you needed me."

Tears sprang to Cece's eyes. With a trembling hand, she lifted the knife from his throat and let it drop with a clatter. When she spoke, she wasn't sure if it was with her voice, or Selena's. Just a girl who'd come to Paris wanting to be loved.

"I was so alone," she whispered, her hips working, an ache building deep inside her. "It was so dark. So cold."

"I know." George's eyes were soft. "Untie me."

Cece fumbled with the ribbons until she freed his limbs, and he sat up to embrace her, folding her into his chest. His lips met hers and they moved together, as one. Cece clutched him, her body tightening around him in a sweet flood of pleasure, and all the fury ran out of her like a retreating river. Perhaps this one was different. Perhaps he wasn't. But she—Cecile Dulac—deserved a chance to find out.

As the glow of orgasm faded, she began to shake.

"I don't—I don't want to go back there."

"You don't have to." George kissed her cheeks. "You have me. Stay with me. Look."

Somebody—Bastian, perhaps, or Rosie—had pulled back the curtains. Sunlight streamed into the ballroom, spilling over Rossignol's still body on the floor, turning everything it touched to gold.

I only wanted to stop them from hurting you, her aunt whispered.

I know. And I'm grateful. But I am not you, and George is not Rossignol.

With a resigned sigh, Selena's spirit untwined itself from her soul and let go, dissolving into the light. In the mirror, Cece caught sight of herself, blonde-haired and blue-eyed once more, and burrowed her face against George's chest, sobbing with relief.

"You won't die tonight," she whispered. "Thank heaven for small mercies."

ABOUT THE AUTHOR

Antonia Rachel Ward is an author of horror and speculative fiction, based in Cambridgeshire, UK. Her short stories and poetry have been published by Blackspot Books, Kandisha Press, and Orchid's Lantern, among others. She is also the founder and editor-in-chief of Ghost Orchid Press.

You can find her on her website, antoniarachelward.com, Instagram @antoniarachelward, or Twitter @antoniarachelw1.

ABOUT THE ILLUSTRATOR

Visual artist Daniella Batsheva is a self-proclaimed "Illustrator with a design habit" whose aesthetic straddles the line between underground and mainstream. Her art boasts the beautiful detail-heavy, intricate linework of the Victorian era mixed with gothic imagery inspired by horror films.

Her art is rooted in the 19th century but with a focus on modernity. Her influences range from Vigee LeBrun to Junji Ito to Camille Rose Garcia. LA is where Daniella found her voice artistically and where her professional work began to really take off. When the pandemic hit, she sought refuge in Palm Desert and eventually made her way to Tel Aviv and London.

She is the Illustrator for storied UK alternative culture brand Kerrang! – helping to usher in a new era of inclusivity through her artworks, she created tour posters and merchandise for Paris Jackson, designed Pizza Girl pasta sauce's labels, and numerous show posters for The Lounge Promotion and Trashville, which have become well-known in London.

Daniella can be found at:
www.daniellabatsheva.com/
www.instagram.com/daniellabatsheva/
www.facebook.com/daniella.batsheva
www.twitter.com/danibatsheva

ACKNOWLEDGEMENTS

Thank you very much to everyone who had a hand in helping turn this book from a rough idea to a polished final draft, especially Joshua Robinson, Jelena Dunato, Lisa Voorhees, Emma K. Leadley, Jessica Wilcox, and April Yates. Your feedback and encouragement was invaluable. Thanks to Elle Turpitt and Stephanie Ellis for helping to polish it into its final form.

This little novella had a bumpy journey to publication, so special thanks to Alex Woodroe for helping to find it a home, and to Heather and Steve of Brigid's Gate for being that home. I couldn't ask for lovelier, more generous people to work with. Also, I must include a huge thank you to Daniella Batsheva for the amazing cover art. It really is a dream come true.

CONTENT WARNINGS

References to suicide.

Domestic violence off page.

Mutilation and violence.

Some sex scenes of dubious consent: a character, while possessed, has numerous sexual encounters.

Misogyny.

Sexism.

Anti-sex-worker sentiment.

MORE FROM BRIGIDS GATE PRESS

Visit our website at: www.brigidsgatepress.com

Paperback ISBN: 978-1-957537-10-8

During the Spring Equinox underneath London, four people enter the caves, but only one will survive. Each trespasser must battle their own demons before facing the White Lady who rises each year to feed on human flesh.

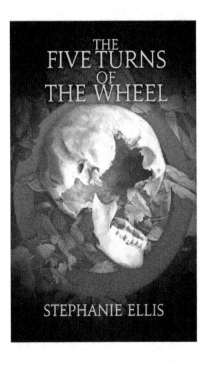

Paperback ISBN: 978-1-957537=21-4

Welcome to the Weald.
The Five Turns of the Wheel has begun.
With each Turn, blood will be spilled,
and sacrifices will be made.
Pacts will be made...and broken.
Will you join the Dance?

In the Weald, the time has come for the Five Turns of the Wheel. Tommy, Betty and Fiddler, the sons of Hweol, Lord of Umbra, have arrived to oversee the sacred rituals...rituals brimming with sacrifice and dripping with blood.

Megan Wheelborn, daughter of Tom my, hatches a desperate plan to free the people of the Weald from the bloody and cruel grip of Umbra, and put an end to its murderous rituals. But success will require sacrifice and blood as well. Will Megan be able to pay the price?

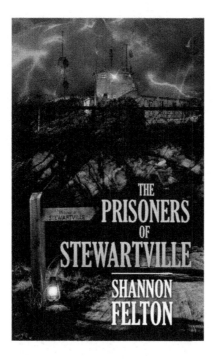

Paperback ISBN: 978-1-957537-31-3

Stewartville. A town living in the shadow of the prisons that drive its economy. Haunted by the ghosts of its past. Cursed by the dark secrets hidden beneath. A town so entwined with the prisons waiting outside the city limits that it's impossible to imagine one without the other, or to ever imagine escaping either.

When a teenage boy digs into the history of the town, he discovers a tunnel system beneath Stewartville, passageways filled with dark secrets. Secrets leading not to freedom, but to un-relenting terror.

Stewartville. Where the convicts aren't the only prisoners.

Paperback ISBN: 978-1-957537-05-4

Arthur, whose life was devastated by the brutal murder of his wife, must come to terms with his diagnosis of dementia. He moves into a new home at a retirement community, and shortly after, has his life turned upside again when his wife's ghost visits him and sends him on a quest to find her killer so her spirit can move on. With his family and his doctor concerned that his dementia is advancing, will he be able to solve the murder before his independence is permanently restricted?

A Man in Winter examines the horrors of isolation, dementia, loss, and the ghosts that come back to haunt us.

Printed in Great Britain
by Amazon

84584020R00072